CW00421055

The Year of the Mask

MARY WEEKS MILLARD

DayOne

© Day One Publications 2022

First printed 2022

ISBN 978-1-84625-732-2

Unless otherwise indicated, Scripture quotations in this publication are taken from the Holy Bible, New International Version (NIV), copyright © 1973, 1978, 1984, 2011 by International Bible Society. Used by permission of Hodder & Stoughton Publishers, A member of the Hodder Headline Group. All rights reserved. "NIV" is a registered trademark of International Bible Society. UK trademark number 1448790.

British Library Cataloguing in Publication Data available

This is a work of fiction. Names, characters, events and incidents are the products of the author's imagination. Any resemblance to actual persons, living or dead, or actual events is purely coincidental.

Published by Day One Publications
Ryelands Road, Leominster, HR6 8NZ

TEL 01568 613 740
FAX 01568 611 473

email—sales@dayone.co.uk

UK web site—www.dayone.co.uk

All rights reserved

No part of this publication may be reproduced, or stored in a retrieval system, or transmitted, in any form or by any means, mechanical, electronic, photocopying, recording or otherwise, without the prior permission of Day One Publications.

Cover design by Kathryn Chedgzoy

Printed by 4Edge

Dedication

For my young friend, Mary.

I hope you enjoy reading this book and it encourages you in your faith.

Acknowledgements

My grateful thanks to DayOne for publishing this book, and especially to Helen Clark for her editing of the manuscript.

My thanks go as always to my ever-patient husband, Malcolm, for all his encouragement, especially when I become tired and discouraged.

I also want to thank the many friends at St. Aldhelm's and St. Ann's Churches, Radipole, Weymouth and the South-West Dorset branch of the Christian Writers' Association who pray for my ministry of writing. Without your prayer support nothing would be accomplished.

– Chapter one –

Devon

'A special assembly is being held this afternoon,' announced Miss Collins, at the end of her history lesson, one Thursday afternoon in March 2020. 'There will be no lessons after the lunch break, but please assemble promptly at 2.00pm in the school hall.'

The girls stood up as she dismissed them and, as soon as she had left the classroom, everyone began asking questions.

'I wonder what it is about?' Song-Wei asked her dorm mate, Annelise. 'It must be important to cancel afternoon school.'

'Perhaps someone has become sick with this new disease that is attacking people in your country,' answered Annelise. 'I haven't watched the news much, but there are lots of rumours going around that there are cases in the UK and that the whole world will be affected.'

The girls made their way to the dining hall, where there was a strange atmosphere of anxiety and excitement. The entire school seemed to be in an upheaval as they collected their meals and began to eat. Everyone wanted to know what was happening, so not one single girl was late finishing her meal and getting to the hall for the assembly.

St. Catherine's was a small boarding school for girls aged eleven to eighteen. It was housed in what had once been a large country manor, set in four acres of woodland in rural Devon. It had been bought and used as a girls' school during the Second World War and continued as such for over seventy years. Most of the girls loved being there. Some, like Annelise, had mothers and elder sisters who had attended the school, and several, like Song-Wei, had been sent from abroad to get an English education.

As the headmistress entered, the whole school became silent—knowing that there must be important news for them to hear.

'Good afternoon, ladies.' Miss Boston greeted them in her usual gentle voice, but her face looked serious.

'As some of you are aware, our country is facing a crisis. It is a medical crisis; we are about to fight a war against an invisible enemy—a virus, called a coronavirus—which is now spreading all over the world. I know that already you have been taught both in your class groups, as well as by matron in your dorms, to be extra careful about washing your hands and I am quite sure you have done that well.'

The girls nodded—many of them had guessed this assembly might be about the pandemic, which governments all around the world were fearing would happen. Maybe they had to have more precautions?

'Our government has issued a warning that from next week our country will be in lockdown. That means that everyone will have to stay at home and keep away from other people, except those who are now termed 'key workers'—people who work in hospitals and other essential services. This means that we must close the school until the crisis is over. This morning

I have been in contact with most of your parents and they will be coming tomorrow to collect you. We have no idea how long this situation will last but you will not be on holiday; you will continue your lessons at home. Your teachers are already planning work, which will be sent to you through the internet and we expect you to be diligent and work just as hard at home as you would in your classes here.

'For those of you who are taking national examinations, we will be hearing from the ministry of education about what will happen. All the staff of St. Catherine's will support you as best we are able.

'What I want you to do now, is collect all your books and personal possessions from your classrooms and go to your dorms to pack your belongings. Mr Peters and his staff will be delivering your cases to your dorms. I doubt very much that you will be returning until after the Easter holidays.

'Those of you who live abroad, can you gather in the prefects' common room and I'll talk to each of you, one by one, about the arrangements your families are making.

'I know this is devastating news, but we will win this war. You must all be brave and sensible, keeping to the rules the government issues, and I am sure we will all be back together again soon.

'This evening, we will have a special meal and a games night—so get packed quickly, in order that we can have fun together later. Please phone your parents and see what time they hope to arrive to take you home or what arrangements they have made.'

Once Miss Boston had dismissed the school, she and the teachers left the assembly hall. The girls all began to chatter and discuss the situation. Annelise felt both excited and scared. Nothing like this had ever happened before in her life. It was sort of like having an unexpected holiday, but then it was so scary that a serious disease was spreading throughout the whole world.

'I have to go to see Miss Boston, so I'll see you back in the dorm later. I wonder if I will be sent home?' Song-Wei commented to Annelise, Daisy and Florence, who were her dorm-mates.

Song-Wei left them and went to the Prefect's common room, while the others made their way to the dorm.

'Do we pack everything?' Daisy asked the others.

'I guess so,' answered Florence. 'We won't need our winter uniform if we don't come back until after Easter. I wonder if my brothers will be sent home from their school, too? It will be fun to have a long time together. We don't see much of each other except in the summer hols.'

In the dorm, they found the cases were by their beds as promised and so began packing.

'I'm changing out of uniform now and I'll wear my jeans and favourite top for this evening. It will almost be like a party. I can wear them when I travel tomorrow,' Annelise told the others. Once she was changed, she remembered that she had to go to the form room and collect her pencil case and other belongings. She made her way back to the main school building and gathered up her belongings from the classroom and then her locker, ready to pack. The dormitories were situated in a separate building nearby. Walking back, she caught sight of Song-Wei, her shoulders drooping and looking very dejected. Annelise hurried to catch her up.

'What's wrong, Song-Wei?' she asked.

'Everything,' her friend replied, trying not to cry. 'It's terrible news—and to make it worse, one of the year nine girls has just spat at me and said horrible things, that it is all because of my country that we have this pandemic.'

'Let's sit out here in the garden for a few minutes and tell me properly what has happened. Are you going back to China, or to your English guardian?' Annelise asked.

'Neither of those,' sobbed Song-Wei. 'Miss Boston told me that my parents are now working up country in the Congo. I knew they were expecting to be sent there. She is unable to contact them because they have no internet or phone signal where they are, and my guardian is locked down in Hong Kong. As school will be closed, she said I would have to go into a children's home—there is nowhere else for me.'

Annelise gasped in horror. 'That's awful! I thought your mum and dad were in China?'

'They were until very recently when the firm Dad works for sent them to the Congo—D.R.C. I think it's called—to supervise building and setting up of a new hospital in a remote place, and Mum will help set up the nursing services there. I knew I wouldn't see them until the summer hols at the earliest, but I had no idea that my guardian, Wong-Jong, had gone to Hong Kong, although she frequently travels there on business for a few days at a time.'

Song-Wei suddenly dissolved into tears. She felt so alone in the world.

'What is a children's home like?' she asked through her sobs. 'Will it be like a prison and will everyone spit at me and hate me because I come from China?'

Annelise put her arm around her friend. She really did not know what to say. She had no idea what it would be like to be in a children's home but didn't like the thought of Song-Wei going there or being bullied.

Then she had an idea. 'I haven't phoned my parents yet, so why don't you go to the classroom and get the things you need, and I'll meet you back at the dorm. We need to pack our cases. I'm sure things will be ok, and it won't be for very long. I'm sure this crisis will soon be over.'

Annelise went to a quiet spot in the garden where she knew she could have privacy and a good reception on her mobile.

'Mum,' she said when her mother answered. 'Before you tell me about the arrangements to collect me, I have a huge favour to ask. Please can Song-Wei come home with me and stay with us until all this is over?'

Annelise heard her mother draw in a deep breath, and before she could answer, she pleaded again. 'You see, her parents have been sent from China to the Congo, her guardian has gone to Hong Kong, and the head said that she would have to go into a children's home until all this is over. Already she's being bullied because she's Chinese and the coronavirus has spread from her country, and her parents are somewhere miles away in a place where they cannot be contacted.'

'Calm down, Annelise,' her mother said. 'I can't get a word in. I hear all you are saying but, and it is a big but, I must ask your father first. He's working at the hospital extra hours due to this emergency, and sleeping there too, in case he brings the virus home. I will speak to him as soon as I can and then get back to you. Be prepared for a 'no' answer if Dad thinks it's not wise. He is a key, frontline worker in this pandemic, and I will take whatever answer he gives. I'm pleased you care about your friend and whatever happens, you can keep in touch by phone and email every day, so tell her that. I expect to be at school around twelve noon tomorrow. Hopefully, I'll speak to you later this evening. Lots of love, sweetheart.'

With that her mother rang off. Annelise sat still for a few minutes. She had so hoped her mum would have said 'yes' at once to her request but, as she thought about it, she knew deep down that her mum was right. Dad was a consultant in the Intensive Care Unit at the Royal United Hospital in Bath, and he would decide what would be best for them all.

With a sigh and a heavy heart, she made her way back to the dorm to finish packing.

– Chapter two –

Devon

The cooks made a fabulous evening meal for everyone—probably trying to use up as much fresh food as they could before the school closed. Then the girls were divided into year groups 7-9 and 10+. They played games together and there was a lot of fun and laughter. In the middle of playing a game of 'Twister', Annelise felt her phone vibrate and then ring. She excused herself and ran into the corridor.

'Hi sweetheart,' her Mum greeted her. 'I've managed to have a word with Dad, and he thinks it would be a great idea if Song-Wei came home with you. It would mean that you would have some company, especially as I expect to be working from home through this crisis and could be very busy.

'I've already spoken to Miss Boston and she is pleased to have a solution to her problem of finding a home for Song-Wei. She is finding her now to tell her the plan. I hope she'll be happy about it.'

'Yay! That's so cool!' Annelise almost shouted down the phone in her delight. 'You'll love her. She's such fun to have around, and very clever. I'm sure she'll help me with my school-work. Thanks a million, Mum!'

Bubbling with excitement, she rushed back into the hall where the girls were playing games. Song-Wei ran up to her and hugged her. 'Miss Boston has just told me the news and I'm so excited and happy! Thank you so much for asking your parents if I could stay with you. I was dreading being sent to a home and praying there would be some other solution where I could be with friends.'

'I phoned Mum as soon as you told me about the home, but I couldn't say anything to you as she had to talk it over with Dad, who at the moment is both working and living at the hospital. He thought it was a great idea.'

The two girls continued to join in the games with smiles all over their faces.

In the dorm that night, it took all four girls a long time to settle. They were excited—it seemed like the holidays had begun early, especially after all the fun and games of the evening—but then, there was fear, too. What did this 'pandemic' mean? How was it that it was closing schools, shops, restaurants, churches, and many other places? As they discussed the situation, Annelise felt shivers of fear as she thought about her father, working day and night in a busy hospital and afraid to come home in case he infected his family. What if he caught the coronavirus himself? Then she thought of Song-Wei and realised it was far worse for her; her parents were somewhere in the wilds of Africa and all her other family members in China where the virus was killing thousands of people. How must she be feeling?

Eventually everyone stopped chatting and one by one the four girls fell asleep.

When the bell rang at 7.00am as usual, Annelise felt tired and a bit disoriented. For a moment she could not understand why her case was at the foot of her bed and her school uniform was not on her chair, ready for the day ahead. Then she remembered; she was going home! Already she could hear Daisy, Florence and Song-Wei pulling back their curtains and rushing out to the bathrooms, so she quickly did the same, grabbing her jeans and top to put on after her shower. In the dorm, each girl had her own space, curtained off to make it private and, as well as a bed, there was a wardrobe, chest of drawers and a bookcase. Annelise's Mum often told her how lucky she was; when she had attended St. Catherine's, the dormitories consisted of a line of twelve beds, with just a locker for each girl and one huge wardrobe which everyone shared.

At breakfast, Matron was clucking around all the girls like a mother hen. She took their temperatures to make sure nobody was sick and so, hopefully, meaning the school was 'virus free'.

She gave the girls letters to take home, explaining to their parents that she must be informed if any of the girls became sick within the next week, so that she could let everyone else know that they would have to self- isolate at home for another ten days. Then she asked the girls to strip their beds before they left.

Cook came into the dining room to ask if anyone needed a packed lunch for their journey, while the school nurse arrived with a big box of face masks.

'If you are travelling on public transport,' she said, 'please wear a mask at all times. If you are going by car, I will still give you one to wear should you have a comfort stop anywhere. It is just a precaution because nobody really knows much about the transmission of this virus. Please, everyone, do remember to wash your hands thoroughly and frequently. If you catch the virus, it might not be serious for you and you may not get many or even any symptoms but you could pass it on to someone else who is more susceptible, and they could become very sick or die. Be responsible. Keep to the rules and government guidelines — stay at home and keep yourselves and everyone around you safe!'

Miss Boston, the headmistress, then spoke to the school.

'I want to wish you all well and tell you to take care of yourselves and those who live near you. As young people you may be able to help elderly neighbours with shopping, if they are unable to go out. Make sure you phone your friends and relatives to keep in touch and always remember to be polite and kind.

'On Monday I want you to log onto St. Catherine's website and follow the link to your class, where you will find work allocated for you. Each weekday, I will expect you to sign into registration and look for your classes. Work will be set for you and we expect you all to email your homework for marking by the time stated. We do not want any of you to fall behind in your grades. If you have problems or worries, you can email the appropriate teacher for help and your parents can phone me during working hours.

'Whenever possible, take an hour's exercise each day as there will be no P. E. or games classes, keeping to the government's guidelines of course. We hope to see you all again soon, maybe after Easter. God bless you all.'

The girls began to leave the dining room. It all sounded so serious and scary. Song-Wei tried to make a joke when the nurse gave her the face mask.

'This is supposed to be the Chinese year of the rat—but now it is the year of the mask!' she said to her dorm mates. They could not help but giggle, but it seemed so serious that they all needed masks.

'I hope we'll all be ok,' Daisy said as they made their way upstairs to strip their beds. 'I live in central London and Mum and Dad say the disease is spreading rapidly and hospitals are already struggling to cope. They are taking me to my grandmother in Kent so that I will be safe. My cousins are also going to be there, so I'll have company, but we'll have to help Nan & Grandpa because they are no longer young.'

'Does that mean you won't see your parents?' asked Florence.

'Well, as Mum said, I wouldn't see them until the Easter hols anyway, so it won't be any different. It'll be cool to hang out with Freddie and Skyla—they're twins and fourteen and we get on well.'

'I wish I had a girl to hang out with,' said Florence. 'I'll just be at home with Mum, Dad and my brothers. My parents will work from home now, but I doubt they'll have much time for me. They both have such important jobs: that's why they sent me here to school, so that I would have friends to hang out with. My brothers are a lot older and we have fun, but they won't want me around all the time, especially as they have GCSE's and A levels this year. I do have a dog, though—Sausage is fun, and I'll get to take him out for walks.'

'I'm so glad I'm going to stay with Annelise,' Song-Wei commented. 'Miss Boston thought I would have to go into a children's home, and I was dreading the thought of that. I wouldn't have known anyone and already some girls here have blamed me because the virus has travelled from China. We'll keep in touch by text and email often and we won't let you feel lonely,' she added.

'That's so mean and crazy,' said Florence. 'You haven't been in China since school started in September. Take no notice of those bullies. We know you didn't bring it over here—it could have started anywhere in the world.'

In the dorm, the girls packed their last few items, exchanged email addresses and phone numbers, stripped their beds and said their goodbyes before going down to the junior common room to wait for their parents.

'We've got time to have a walk in the woods,' Annelise suggested to Song-Wei, glancing at her watch. 'Mum promised to text when she is almost here. I want to go to the pond and say goodbye to the baby moorhens.'

'Yay! That would be cool,' replied Song-Wei. 'I'll take a photo—I've already decided to keep a diary while we are in this lockdown—maybe one day my parents will be able to read it,' she said, wiping a tear from her eye. Annelise put her arm around her friend's shoulder. 'I'm sure they'll be fine, and you'll be able to see them after the summer term.'

'I hope and pray every night that it will be ok, but I'm not sure that Dad's work will allow me to visit them in the Congo—it's a country with a lot of fighting between tribes and has the Ebola disease in places. I might be able to visit my grandparents in China, though, but if not, I will be in London with my guardian. Wong-Jong is like an auntie to me and very kind.'

– CHAPTER THREE –

Somerset

'That's Mum texting,' said Annelise, hearing her phone give its jingle. 'Let's get back to the common room. It's so cool you are coming home with me—we'll have fun. You'll love our dog, Goldie—he's very friendly, and loves going out for walks.'

Half an hour later the girls were getting into the car and starting the journey from Devon to Higher Summerfield—a village to the south-west of Bath. Song-Wei was introduced to Mrs Lacey and she politely thanked her for allowing her to stay with Annelise. She felt shy and unsure about family life in England. This was her first year in an English school and the half term breaks and Christmas holiday she had spent in London with her guardian. Mrs Lacey was also feeling just a little apprehensive because she had no idea of Chinese culture and very much wanted her young guest to feel at home and be happy.

'Have you ever visited Bath?' she asked. 'It is an amazing city with many historic buildings to see.'

'No, Mrs Lacey, I have only stayed in London and at school,' Song-Wei answered. 'I think I would like to visit Bath.'

'That's good,' Annelise's Mum answered. 'We can have a trip there one day when we are allowed out again. Maybe we can also go to Weston-Super-Mare as well. It's a seaside town. Have you been to the sea?'

'No, never. We live far from the coast in China. I flew over the ocean to come to Britain but didn't see it. That would be cool, thank you,' Song-Wei answered.

'You'll love it staying with us,' said Annelise. 'We'll do all sorts of things and you can write it up in your diary.' Then, she explained to her Mum that Song-Wei planned on making a 'lockdown' diary with photos, so that her parents could see what she was doing in this strange time.

'I think you should make one as well, Annelise. You are living through a special time in history. Nothing like this has happened for centuries. You can make a scrapbook with newspaper cuttings so that people in future generations will be able to understand what happened.'

Mrs Lacey stopped the car and parked in a beautiful picnic area outside Exeter.

'I thought we could have our picnic lunch here; it's such a pretty place,' she told the girls. They were glad to get out and walk around. They walked by the river, before finding a bench where they could sit and eat.

Song-Wei began to feel a little less shy of Annelise's mum and enjoyed the fun of a picnic by the river.

'I'm so glad that you are staying with us,' Mrs Lacey told her. 'I will be working at home most days but may not have much time to spend with you girls, as normally someone comes to help me each week with the housework. With the new regulations of social distancing, she has decided not to come until after the crisis is over. I shall have to do all the cleaning and cooking now, as well as my work, and I'm not used to that!'

'Mum,' said Annelise at once, 'we can help, too. We won't be doing schoolwork all day long.'

'Thanks, I'll take you up on that offer, I'm sure. Well, if we have all had enough to eat, we must get back on the road,' she answered.

It wasn't too long before they arrived in Higher Summerfield village. Song-Wei had her face glued to the car window as they drove down the narrow high street and then up a hill and into the drive of what seemed to be a large house. It was old, built of stone, with a large doorway, double -fronted windows and three stories high. She felt a little scared as it was so imposing and so different to the block of apartments where she lived with her parents in China.

'Welcome to our home,' Mrs Lacey said to her. 'We hope you'll be very happy staying with us while school is closed.'

'Thank you,' replied Song-Wei. 'It's so kind of you to invite me. I was scared at the thought of going into a children's home, and it was horrible thinking that nobody wanted me.' She wiped a tear from her eye, hoping that no one had seen it.

The front door opened and out came a young man. Annelise ran over to him and they hugged each other.

'Mummy didn't tell me you were home—that's so cool!' she shouted. 'Will, come and meet my school friend, Song-Wei.' Mrs Lacey laughed. 'I thought it would be a nice surprise for you.

William is home for the weekend, before the lockdown starts officially.'

William smiled at Song-Wei, as she was introduced to Annelise's brother. He normally lived in Leeds working as a junior doctor in a large general hospital. He was very tall, with bright blue eyes which twinkled as he smiled at her.

'I'll bring your cases in,' he said. 'The kettle is on. I'm sure you are longing for a cup of tea.'

As they entered the large hallway, a beautiful golden retriever came rushing over to them.

'Oh Goldie,' exclaimed Annelise, bending down to bury her face in the dog's silky hair. 'I've missed you so much. We'll have lots of walks together now I'm home!' Song-Wei was not very used to dogs, but soon found that Goldie was gentle and wanted to be her friend, so began petting him, too.

'Come into the kitchen and we'll have a drink. Then we'll show you your room,' Mrs Lacey said, leading Song-Wei down a corridor and into a large, sunny kitchen. 'When we are on our own, we use this as our family hub, and we eat here, too. It is much cosier than the dining room, especially in the winter. This is a big house and has far more rooms than we need, but we love living here. Isobel, Annelise's older sister is a nurse, working on a research project in The Gambia. We have been trying to arrange a flight home for her, as this terrible virus is spreading all over the world, and we feel she would be safer here. So, you may get to meet her, too.'

Song-Wei found her shyness melting away as the family chatted to her and made her feel at home.

– CHAPTER FOUR –

Somerset

Song-Wei almost cried when she saw the bedroom where she was to sleep. It was the biggest bedroom in which she had ever slept. The window looked out over the back garden and had pink, striped curtains which matched the bed linen. By her bed was a small table and Mrs Lacey had picked some primroses and put them in a little vase, along with a pile of story books for her to read. Her room was next to Annelise's bedroom on the top floor. Annelise told her that when she had been small, it had been the nursery. What used to be a playroom was now a study and would serve the girls as a classroom where they could do their schoolwork each day. There was a large bookcase in that room with many more interesting books.

The girls shared a bathroom, and what had once been a sitting room for a nanny, was now a snug with a television for them.

There were two more rooms on the top floor, both of which had been used in Georgian times as servant's bedrooms, but now were used to store all sorts of odds and ends.

'Mum and Dad sleep on the floor below us, as do Will and Isobel when they are at home. Then, there is a guest room and a family bathroom. Mum and Dad and Isobel have their own ensuite bathrooms, too,' Annelise explained when she gave her a tour of the house.

'It's like a palace!' Song-Wei exclaimed. 'It's an amazing old house. I really like it, for it seems to say "welcome" to you when you come inside.'

'I love it here. We all do, and even though we no longer need such a big house, we decided not to down-size. Will and Isobel are rarely here now but, as Dad says, it is their home until they have their own. We know we are very blessed to live here, but the downside is that Mum and Dad have high-powered jobs and work long hours and they will have to keep doing so, because it takes a lot of money for the upkeep. We don't see each other as much as we would like. That's why I was sent to St. Catherine's—so that I wouldn't be lonely.'

'I was sent to St. Catherine's for a very different reason,' explained Song-Wei. 'Life in China is hard for people like my parents who have become Christians. When I was born there was still a "one child" policy in the country. Parents were allowed only one child, in order to reduce the ever- increasing birth rate. After my birth, my parents and grandparents all began to save what money they could to send me abroad to a boarding school in a country where Christianity is totally accepted. Although there is freedom of religion stated in the constitution of China and there are some state approved Christian churches, many of the Chinese people feel that if we are not good Communist party members then we are not good citizens. They give Christians a hard time.

'My parents want me to get a good education but also to learn to think about political and religious issues for myself and make

25

my own mind up about things. From a small child I was taught to speak in English as well as Mandarin, to prepare me for a school in England or America.

'Auntie Wong-Jong, my guardian in London, used to live in our local community in China, and it was she who taught me to read and write in English. When I was eleven, she found a school for me to attend and has been like an auntie to me. I am so grateful for all the sacrifices people have made for me to come to school,' Song-Wei told Annelise, looking a little sad because home seemed so far away.

'Hi girls', called out Will as he climbed the stairs to the top floor. 'I'm going to take Goldie out for a walk. Would you like to come?'

'Yes please,' they chorused together.

'Then get your coats and meet me in the hall in five minutes. It still gets dark early these days, so we need to make the most of the afternoon.'

Will wanted a little time with his young sister and her friend. As a doctor, he knew how serious the coronavirus pandemic might prove to be and without scaring the girls, he felt he needed to explain a few things to them. He had no idea when he would be able to come home again as these were such uncertain times.

'We'll show you the garden, Song-Wei,' said Will, 'because much of the time for the next few weeks you will be confined to the house and garden. We are so blessed here because we have a large house and a lot of ground.'

They went out of the back door and Song-Wei gasped at the lovely garden in front of them. 'I don't know how much Annelise has told you about us,' Will remarked, 'but we are quite an outdoors-loving family. We do have a gardener to help with this part of the garden,' he continued, leading them through a gate in a wall into the walled kitchen garden. 'His name is Bill, but he is elderly, and we have decided that he ought not to come to help during lockdown. As spring is coming, you might like to help when you can to keep things tidy. How do you feel about that?'

'We'll do our best,' answered Annelise. 'I used to help Bill before I went to St. Catherine's.'

'I've always lived in an apartment, but I'd love to learn about plants,' added Song-Wei.

'That's great, and a weight off my mind,' replied Will. 'I'm worried about Mum getting worn out. Her work will be in even greater demand during this crisis, and she has always had help with the house and garden. Annelise, please text me often and let me know how things are going, because Dad will also be very busy and not able to come home, in case he brings infection here. Isobel may or may not get home—she's told me that she thinks she should stay and help if the pandemic spreads to The Gambia, and I agree with her.'

Goldie ran ahead of them as they left the walled garden through another gate and entered a wooded area.

'I love our woods,' said Annelise to Song-Wei. 'I used to play here so much when I was small. I still have a tree house near the swimming pool.'

'You have your own swimming pool?' asked Song-Wei in amazement.

'Yes, we do,' answered Will. 'Normally it is closed until Easter, but I have talked with Dad and he has said that if you are willing to do the maintenance each week, then you may use it for your daily exercise.'

'We will,' shouted Annelise, delight all over her face. 'Show me what I need to do.'

They raced through the woods to a clearing, and Song-Wei saw, what at first looked like a large marquee, with a wooden house beside it.

'This is our pool,' explained Annelise. 'I didn't think we could use it, so I didn't tell you about it.'

Will took out a key from his pocket and unlocked the door of the wooden hut. They went inside and he showed Song-Wei the changing rooms, shower and tiny kitchen where they would be able to make hot drinks. Then he showed them the controls for the water temperature and the disinfectant which needed to be added every week. He taught them how to test the water before they added the solution. Song-Wei loved chemistry, so she was very quick to understand what they had to do, though it was all written clearly on a poster on the wall in case they forgot.

'Annelise knows all the safety rules about using the pool, so she can explain those. I will be happy if you never come here on your own—only together or with Mum.'

The girls nodded, promising they would keep the rules.

'Just one other thing, before we go back to the house. Do you know how to ride a bike, Song-Wei?' he asked.

'Yes,' she answered, 'Though not very well.'

'That's good,' Will told her. 'Tomorrow, I'll get Isobel's bike out of the garage and see if you can manage it—then the three of us can have a bike ride and you can see the village.'

Song-Wei looked at Annelise, trying to keep the tears back. She felt overwhelmed at all the kindness she was being shown and this seemed to her like the most marvellous holiday she had ever had.

'Thank you so much for all your kindness—I feel overwhelmed. If only my parents could know that I am in such a lovely place with kind people.'

– CHAPTER FIVE –

Somerset

Everyone was determined to make the weekend special. There was a foreboding about what the new week would bring, as lockdown regulations were to be imposed and with no knowledge of when they might end.

Mrs Lacey was worried. She hoped she had done the right thing by taking in someone else's daughter—what if Song-Wei contracted the virus and became sick, or even worse, died?

She also feared for her husband and adult children, all of whom were key workers in the medical field and so would be at greater risk of catching the virus. The pandemic seemed like a curse on the whole world. Would it herald the end of the world? That terrifying thought also crossed her mind. She had never in adult life been interested in religion, although if asked, she would classify herself as a Christian. Maybe it was time to think about these things, for in her work as a counsellor and stress management consultant, even with all her degrees and expertise, she was aware she did not have all the answers when people came to her with their problems.

Will fixed up the bike for Song-Wei, found a spare helmet, and then took the girls into the village. They were going to see if they could buy some toilet rolls and flour from the village shop, as these commodities had suddenly become scarce with people stockpiling what they thought were essentials. Mrs Lacey was busy making a picnic, planning to take everyone into Bath while there was still an opportunity to do so. The strict regulations were due to come into force in the middle of the coming week.

Song-Wei soon began to gain confidence on the bike. Higher Summerfield was a small village with quiet roads—ideal for cyclists, especially inexperienced ones like her.

'Well, hello,' Maggie, the shopkeeper, greeted them when they arrived. It was a lovely shop, stocking almost everything the villagers might need. Once it had been a Post Office as well, but now everyone had to go to the nearby town of Paulton if they needed those services, but Maggie still stocked stamps and there was a pillar box outside.

'So, you have come home from school, Annelise, and I guess this is a school friend?' she asked.

'Yes, Maggie. This is Song-Wei, and she isn't able to go home to her parents so is staying with us. We'll have fun together and I'll have company.'

'That's cool,' Maggie commented, 'and Dr Will, it's good to see you, too. Are you home to stay, as well?'

'Sadly not, Maggie. I'm back to Leeds tomorrow evening. This is just a quick break before lockdown starts as it's unlikely staff will be allowed leave through the pandemic. No one really knows how many people will become infected or how long it might last. We've just come for a few essentials. Mum says everyone is buying flour and toilet rolls, so thought maybe we should have some more, if you have any to spare?' Will answered.

'I've kept some for my regular customers. I'm rationing them, but you can have a kilo of flour and a packet of nine toilet rolls. As soon as we get new stocks in, then I'll put some aside for my regulars. 'It's only fair,' she told them.

Delighted with their purchases the trio began to cycle home, stopping on the way to show Song-Wei the church and the village hall, which once had been a small school. The local children now were picked up by a bus and taken to Paulton for primary school.

By the time they had arrived back at Barrow House, Mrs Lacey had everything ready for their trip to Bath.

'I've been thinking,' she said to Song-Wei. 'Maybe you could call me Julia, rather than Mrs Lacey, which sounds so formal.'

Song-Wei was quiet for a few minutes before she answered.

'I would be happy to call you Aunt Julia,' she replied. 'You see, in my culture it would be rather rude to call you only by your first name. Would that be alright?'

'Of course, Song-Wei, and I quite understand. I was brought up to call all my parents' friends of the older generation "aunt" or "uncle". I'm sure that my husband would rather you called him "Uncle James" rather than Dr Lacey.'

The four of them were soon settled in the car and on the way to Bath. It was only about eight miles away. The countryside was still mostly in winter mode, but there were a few green leaves coming out on some trees and snowdrops and primroses in the hedgerows, which glistened in the sun.

'We will not explore Bath today because of the coronavirus,' Will told the girls, for he was driving. 'But I'll give you a tour of the city skyline and then point out some places as we drive around to the north side. We plan to have our picnic in the Victoria Park, in front of the Royal Crescent.'

Will was good at explaining things to Song-Wei and she was enchanted by some of the lovely old buildings. Once they had found a parking place, they helped carry the picnic things into the park.

'We'll head for the bandstand. It will be a good place to sit,' Will instructed. 'There's only one person sitting there and I'm sure he won't mind us joining him. In fact, he looks quite friendly!'

Annelise looked over and screamed with delight. 'It's Dad!' and ran to him, jumping into his arms.

Song-Wei felt shy and was not quite sure what to do or say, so hung behind the others. Will realized and waited for her to catch him up. Then he told her that it had been planned as a surprise for them all, as their father wouldn't be able to see them very often once the restrictions were all in place after the weekend.

It was a noisy, happy picnic—a real celebration together. Doctor Lacey was full of fun and glad that Song-Wei wanted to call him 'Uncle James', so he could forget he was a doctor and all the pressures on him for an hour or two. They played rounders together as best as they were able with only five people—it helped to keep them warm as it was still early March. As the light began to fade, they packed up everything and prepared to go home.

'I need to talk to you all seriously,' Dr Lacey said. 'This has been a great time, but the pandemic is spreading rapidly, and we all need to take the government's advice and be extremely careful. Higher Summerfield may seem a hundred miles away from any infection, but viruses spread rapidly, and no one can be one hundred per cent sure they will stay safe.

'Look after each other and those around you. Will and I will be out there on the front line, so to speak, fighting this war against the disease. Isobel has also now decided to stay in West Africa and help there while she is needed. I'm so glad you girls are home to help Mum, because she'll be busy with her work. I know you will do your schoolwork, too. I'll be messaging and phoning when I can and I'm sure Will and Isobel will do the same. Now, no tears—just one last hug and I must go back to the hospital.'

It was hard for everyone to stay cheerful, but Will soon organized the girls to carry things to the car and promised them a moonlight swim that evening.

- CHAPTER SIX -

The Ituri Forest in north-east Congo

It was dark soon after 6pm—an eerie darkness that Lydia could not quite get used to. It seemed to her that one moment it was still light, then suddenly the sun disappeared, and the deep darkness wrapped itself around everyone and everything. The noises of the animals in the trees and bushes, which had sounded benign through the day, now made her shiver and feel scared.

'Don't be so silly,' she said to herself. 'We have only lived here for a few weeks; you will get used to it.' Lydia lit a hurricane lantern and hung it outside on the porch, to welcome her husband home from work. A gecko scuttled up the wall, making her jump as it raced after an insect, which would no doubt make it a good supper.

Thinking about supper, she returned to the kitchen to stir the soup which she was making for their evening meal. She sang as she did so—a song praising God that He was with her always, wherever she was and whatever she was doing.

She heard the noise of a truck driving over the bumpy mud road and then saw the glow of the head lights as it drove up in front of the house. What a welcome sight! Lydia ran to the veranda and greeted her husband, John, with a hug. She found the hours while he was at work a little lonely, even though she kept herself busy trying to learn both French and Kingwana, the local form of Swahili.

'How was your day, my love?' she asked John as he took off his cap and hung it in the porch.

'Good, darling, all good,' he said to his wife with a smile. 'I have something for you,' and he handed over a small packet.

'We have mail from China!' she shouted in delight. 'There is a letter from my parents and one from Hong Kong—but nothing from England.' Lydia's face fell for a moment, sad that there was no letter from Song-Wei.

'The boss flew up from Kinshasa today, bringing mail for quite a lot of the workforce, but a couple of guys were very disappointed because there was nothing for them,' he told her.

Lydia tore open the envelopes, thrilled to get news. Her husband's parents had died some years before, but her own parents lived in an apartment near to theirs, in the same large industrial town in the centre of China. Almost everyone called them Grandma and Grandpa Lee. They had helped with childcare for Song-Wei before she left to go to school in England and were missing all their family very much.

'My mother writes that the coronavirus (Covid-19), is spreading rapidly and many people are sick. The government have asked the Christians to send workers to help, even older people like them. They have volunteered, and she is going to work as a cook and father as a porter in a large hospital which has just been built to deal only with Covid-19 patients. Several others from the church family are also going. Other neighbours are saying they are mad, but Mother has told them that, as Christians, they are not afraid of dying, because they have a home in heaven with Jesus. She does say that everyone is missing us, and asking how Pastor John and Lydia are getting on in Africa and when will we be going home?'

'That's a good question,' answered John. 'The boss has put a suggestion to me, which we need to pray about and find out what God wants us to do.'

'Whatever do you mean, John?' Lydia asked, looking puzzled. 'We are here only for a few months, surely?'

John took a deep breath and put his arm around his wife. He knew that she was not finding it easy living in the Ituri forest, far from civilization. There was a little airstrip, and some very poor mud roads to the village where they were working, but with no electricity, running water, internet connections or phones, apart from the short-wave radio, they had no regular connection with the outside world.

'I have been asked to consider staying here for a couple of years, as hospital administrator, and there would be work for you to continue as a sister as soon as you have the nursing services up and running. Most of the guys will return to China. Maybe just a couple might want to stay on as maintenance workers. I must admit, I was shocked at first, but as I have thought about it through the day, I can see some advantages as well as the disadvantages.'

Lydia trembled in his arms. Thoughts raced through her head—what about Song-Wei? What about her parents? What about the little church which met in their home and John pastored? What about the insects, snakes and other things she hated here? Could she live in the tropical forest for years?

'What advantages can you see?' Lydia asked, tears forming in her eyes.

'Here we are not dominated by the Communist party and that feeling of being despised because we are Christians. We could share the good news about Jesus with the forest Pygmies and meet with the local church, once our language skills have improved.

We live in the beautiful forest, with clean air. We don't need to wear masks when we go out because of air pollution. Think how much better your asthma has been since we came here! In fact, we don't need masks because of Covid-19 either because it's unlikely it will reach this remote place. We will both have satisfying jobs with good salaries and that will help with Song-Wei's education.'

Lydia was quiet for a few minutes, thinking about what her husband was saying.

'I understand those things,' she answered, 'and they are good. But what about Song-Wei? Would she still be able to come home for her long holiday? How can we care for my parents should they become sick and need us?'

'My boss explained that, as expatriates working here long-term, there would be certain extra allowances for us to return each year for a long holiday in China. We can arrange to go from time to time to Bunia for shopping or even over to Uganda. We would be provided with a four-by-four vehicle for our personal use. I think we should spend some time praying about the proposal. We don't have to decide for a month until the boss visits again.'

Lydia felt calmer after they had prayed—she knew that God would show them what they should do. She prayed, too, that if they were to stay, God would help her conquer her fears, and to speak the language more fluently.

Over their evening meal, John told her all the other news that the supervisor had brought.

'We are ahead of the schedule with some things,' he told her. 'The engineers have done so well with harnessing the water from the waterfall, that we should have electricity to the hospital site very soon, and then they will bring it down to our houses here in the village. The hospital should be completed in a month or so—or enough to admit urgent cases—and then you can begin working with patients. The boss told me that the Covid-19 rate of infection is now high in Europe, so we must pray that Song-Wei and her school do not become infected. It seems that children and young people often have no symptoms even if they do test positive.'

– CHAPTER SEVEN –

News from Hong Kong and China.

With so much to think about and talk over, Lydia had forgotten to open the letter she had received from Hong Kong. It was not until she was in bed, tucked under the mosquito net and ready for John to turn out the hurricane lamp, that she remembered about it.

'Oh dear!' she exclaimed. 'I haven't opened the other letter. Can you wait a few minutes while I get it?'

'I'll get it for you,' John said, extricating himself from under the net and finding a torch to guide him into the living room. As he went, he heard the guard walking outside and their faithful dog, Shenzi, padding along beside him. John smiled. It was good to know they were being looked after, and he called out, 'usiku njema!' to wish the guard a good night.

Once back in bed, Lydia and John read the letter eagerly—it was so good to get news. The letter was from Wong-Jong, their daughter's guardian.

'I have come over to Hong Kong to visit friends and business,' she wrote, 'and I tried to phone you in China, only to discover from Grandma Lee that you are both in the middle of Africa! Keep well and stay safe while you are there. I wanted you to know that Song-Wei had a very good first term at St. Catherine's and her report was excellent from every teacher. She is working hard, excelling in her violin lessons and only English is still a weak subject. She seems to love the school and shares a dormitory with three other girls, all of whom are friendly and helpful to her. We had a lovely Christmas together, and she enjoyed visiting the Chinese Church which I attend. I am sure her letters will have told you all about her new life.

I expect to be in Hong Kong until early February. Then I will be back for Song-Wei's half-term holiday but will have to return here afterwards to complete a business deal.

'We are all being careful on the island about wearing masks and handwashing, because this terrible new virus has spread here from the mainland, but so far it seems to be contained.'

The parents thanked God for such a loving guardian, who had known Song-Wei most of her life and had taught them all some English when she had lived near them in China. Even though Lydia was sad there was no letter from her daughter in the mail, she was thrilled to get good news.

Meanwhile, in China, life was changing for Grandma and Grandpa Lee. Now into their seventies it seemed strange to be returning to work, but the need in their country was so great. The virus had spread rapidly, and thousands of people were falling sick with many dying. A new hospital had been built and equipped in just a couple of weeks, so urgent was the need. When the small Christian community had been asked to help, the Lees were happy to volunteer. As Christians they were often regarded in a poor light by their Communist neighbours, who were suspicious of their activities and criticized them for not being good citizens because they did not belong to the Communist Party. So, they saw this as a way to show them they cared about their country and community and were willing to help.

As they both did shift work, they were offered a room on the hospital campus, which they accepted. This kept them isolated and less likely to spread the virus in their home community.

Grandma Lee had always loved cooking and she was in her element in the large kitchen, and did not mind what she did, from preparing vegetables to washing dishes. Very soon she became respected by the people working with her, most of whom called her 'grandma'.

Grandpa Lee worked as a porter, and he, too, in spite of his age, was an energetic and willing helper. The long hours made them both tired, but they felt strongly that this is what God wanted them to do to show the people around them that God existed and loved them. It also helped them to cope as they were missing Lydia and John as well as their granddaughter.

'Song -Wei will be thirteen soon. Imagine her being a teenager!' Grandma Lee commented to her husband one evening after work. 'I hope she is happy and remembers that all the family pray for her every day. I am longing for the summer holidays when everyone will be back home again.'

'I long for that, too,' replied Grandpa Lee, 'but it is feared that this virus will spread all over the world and this could be a difficult year. I think it should be called "year of the mask" as everyone now has to wear a mask at all times outside of their home, instead of being 'the year of the rat.'"

'I fear that even masks, handwashing and distancing may not control this virus,' answered his wife, 'but we have hope because we know we are in God's hands, as is our family. I pray for the people around us who have no hope should they or their loved ones die. I pray we can be shining lights in the darkness.'

The next day, the darkness seemed to close in more than ever, as Grandpa Lee felt unwell and went to be tested for Covid-19. When the test returned positive, he was admitted to a ward and Grandma sent to stay isolated in her room for ten days, with food being left outside her door, and almost no contact with anyone. This was a real test of her faith, all alone, not allowed to visit her husband, not even getting news of how he was faring. Would this darkness put out the light in her heart or take away her hope?

- CHAPTER EIGHT -

Somerset

The girls soon settled into a routine—Mrs Lacey had decided that it would be best for Annelise and Song-Wei to have set times for all their activities, just as they would have had at school.

After breakfast they took Goldie for a walk in the garden, whatever the weather. Then they went to the old playroom and settled down to do their schoolwork for that morning, having a twenty-minute break halfway through, before continuing to work until lunchtime. To be helpful, Annelise and Song-Wei had decided to take it in turns to make lunch for the three of them.

In the afternoon, they either had P.E. using an exercise class they had discovered on the internet, went to the pool for a swim, or cycled in the garden. Then the girls had time to do some art, textiles, or cookery for an hour before the end of their 'school day'.

Sometimes their lessons were on a social media platform where they were able to see their classmates and teachers, but at other times they worked quietly doing set projects. Song-Wei was excellent at maths, whereas Anneliese struggled with that subject but was better at English, as that was a second language for her friend, so they helped each other.

'Thanks so much for helping me with my maths,' Annelise said to Song-Wei one morning. 'I've always hated it and felt so stupid when I couldn't get things right. I'm the dumb one of the family. Both my brother and sister have done very well, but I'm just useless and haven't any idea what I will do with my life. I'm sure I won't be clever enough to go to university; sometimes I get so depressed about it all. I think I was an 'accident' coming so long after the other two, when Mum was getting back into her career. I probably wasn't really wanted, but she got landed with me. Sometimes I feel I'm a big disappointment to my parents.'

Annelise looked so sad that Song-Wei gave her a big hug.

'I felt a bit like that once,' she said. 'In our country, at the time when I was born, couples were only allowed one child by law, to keep the population down. If a mother was found to be pregnant a second time, then she was forcibly taken to a hospital and an abortion performed.'

'Oh, that's terrible!' exclaimed Annelise.

'Yes, it was,' answered Song-Wei, 'and everyone was so thankful when the law was changed from the 'One Child Policy'. At that time, most people in China wanted the one child to be a son, because sons would support parents in their old age and were thought to be more important than daughters. So, I grew up thinking my parents were disappointed in me because I was born the 'wrong' sex.'

'Do you still feel like that?' asked Annelise.

'No, I don't,' she replied, her eyes shining. 'I know that I am loved and treasured and there is a purpose to my life.'

'I wish I felt like that,' said her friend, sadly. 'Sometimes I feel just a waste of space. I'm not pretty, not good at sports, music, art, schoolwork; I'm not even 'average', just the bottom set for almost everything.'

'I'll tell you sometime what changed things for me, but just now I must go to the kitchen. It's my turn to get lunch,' said Song-Wei, as she put her books away.

Annelise went with her and helped to set the table.

While they were eating lunch, Mrs Lacey told the girls that she needed to visit her office in Bath that afternoon.

'Sorry to leave you on your own,' she said. 'What will you be doing?'

'I would like to swim today,' decided Annelise. 'Are you ok with that?' she asked her friend.

'Oh yes, that's cool,' she responded. 'Afterwards I could cook the evening meal for you Aunt Julia, if that would be helpful?'

'That would be fantastic,' answered Mrs Lacey, who did not much like cooking and knew she might be late home. 'Just look in the fridge and find something. I don't mind what you cook. I should be home in time for us to eat at six. Thanks so much, girls.'

When Mrs Lacey had gone, Annelise turned to Song-Wei.

'Whatever made you suggest that? I don't know how to cook a proper meal, do you?'

Song-Wei laughed. 'Don't panic. In the part of China where I live, all girls learn to cook. My grandmother taught me. Let's look in the fridge and see what we can find. I hope there's some rice in the store cupboard and do you know where your mum keeps her spices?' They had a good look around before they went to swim and Song-Wei found things that she could use to make a meal.

Both girls could swim well and the hour in the pool passed very quickly. They showered and dressed, and then returned to the house to start work in the kitchen.

'Today girls, we will cook sweet and sour prawns with stir fry vegetables and egg fried rice,' Song-Wei announced in a loud voice, trying to imitate Miss Gray, their Home Economics mistress at school. Annelise giggled.

'Get your notebook and write down the ingredients and then I will instruct you how to cook this Chinese speciality. You will write the recipe down, so that you will remember how to cook it. Go and wash your hands and put on your aprons.'

Annelise ran upstairs and brought down their cookery aprons, and her pen and notebook.

'I want to learn properly. It will be so cool to cook a Chinese meal when Dad gets home. He loves Chinese food.'

'I'll do my best to teach you, but we will have to use the spices your mum has. I'll tell you what I would use at home, so when you do it for yourself you can try to get the proper ones,' Song-Wei told her.

The rest of the afternoon went so quickly. First, they prepared all the vegetables—very carefully as they sliced them thinly. The rice was weighed out and rinsed. Then the prawns were shelled and cleaned. They were so occupied that they did not hear Mrs Lacey return and jumped when she opened the kitchen door.

'Wow, you look busy,' she said. 'I'll leave you to get on with the meal and come down at six. Bless you.'

Song-Wei proved to be a good teacher and Annelise was really interested and learnt quickly.

They chatted as they cooked together and then set the table as nicely as they could, even putting a bunch of primroses from the garden in a vase.

'This is so good, much nicer than from the take-away!' Mrs Lacey said in genuine amazement. You are very talented, Song-Wei.'

'We both did it. We pretended it was a cookery lesson at school and used my grandma's recipe. Annelise did as much as I did. We just had to manage without a few spices, but we are glad you liked it.'

'Liked it? I loved it, and so will Uncle James when he comes home. Tell me the spices you need, and I'll order them with my next grocery order. I think we may have to have a Chinese evening every week. After the meal you can tell us about your life in China—that is, if you would like to do so.'

'Oh yes!' answered Song-Wei, 'but only if we have an English evening on another day, so that you can tell me more about the English culture. I would like that please.'

It seemed such a good idea to have these special evenings, that they incorporated them into the routine, but chose to have 'British' rather than just English evenings, since Mrs Lacey had been brought up in Scotland, and also had Irish ancestry. Annelise chose dishes for the British evenings and found recipes in a cookery book which her mother had on the shelf, but rarely used. She discovered that she enjoyed cooking and the girls had loads of fun working together. Mrs Lacey was quite amazed at how well the girls managed and what delicious meals they produced.

– Chapter nine –

Somerset

The first few weeks of lockdown passed quickly. By April the weather was warm and dry, and the girls were able to go out and about on their bikes. It was officially school holiday time, so there were no online lessons, and there were many places to explore in the surrounding area. Sometimes the girls took a picnic lunch with them. Goldie loved long walks with the girls, especially when they went near the river where he could swim and cool off.

Annelise loved the occasional weekends when her dad was free to come home for an hour or so, but he always stayed in the garden, socially distanced from them. The virus was spreading rapidly, and many people were dying. It was terrible to hear the official announcements on the television each afternoon.

One day, they learnt that Will was sick with the Covid-19 virus. He was in intensive care in the hospital where he worked in Leeds and struggling to breathe. Annelise's father was in constant contact with the hospital and relayed the news each day to his wife. They all understood that he was so sick he could die, and it was frightening, especially not being able to see him.

Song-Wei tried to comfort Annelise and Mrs Lacey. She knew what she should do but was scared she might be laughed at if she suggested it. One afternoon the news was so bad and

Annelise and her mum were sitting in the snug their eyes red from crying.

'Please Aunt Julia,' she said very hesitantly. 'Please will you let me pray for you and Will? You know my father is a pastor and has taught me to pray in every situation.'

Annelise looked a little surprised but her mother reached out and took Song-Wei's hand, and answered, 'Please do. I am not a church goer and don't know much about God, but I do believe there is a God who made this universe, and if He can help in this desperate time, please ask Him!'

'I'll speak in Mandarin,' she told them, 'because it is my heart language and I think in Mandarin.'

She began to pray softly and although Annelise and her Mum could not understand the words, they both sensed a peace around them and felt calmer. When Song-Wei stopped, they said, 'Amen.'

'Thank you, dear,' said Mrs Lacey. 'Perhaps we can pray again before we go to bed. I feel calmer now.'

Over the following days, although the news from the hospital was neither better nor worse, God's peace seemed to fill the home and they felt a hope which had not previously been there.

Song-Wei wished she could explain more about knowing God as a loving father and talking to Him about everything, but it was hard to put what she wanted to say into another language. She found more and more she was talking to God when she was alone or out in the garden, on a walk in the countryside. She prayed for Will, for the family who had given her a home, and for her family so far away in the Congo and China. She longed to hear news of them. Were they sick? Were they still alive? Would she ever see them again?

On their next Chinese evening, Song-Wei cooked her Grandma Lee's favourite chicken dish.

After they had eaten, she began to talk about China, not just about the culture and the town where she lived, but about her family and their beliefs and how they were considered not to be good Chinese citizens because of their faith. Annelise and her mum had no idea how difficult it could be to live in a country where Christians were a minority. No wonder her parents had saved all the money they could to send Song-Wei to have an education other than in a state school where Communism was taught.

'Why do you have a Chinese name and not a Christian name like your parents and grandparents?' Annelise asked her.

'Before I left China, I decided that I would be a follower of Jesus, and I do talk to Him every day and read my Bible, but I was not brave enough to be baptized and take a Christian name. Now I wish I had been stronger in my faith and done that, because I know that my family could be in danger of losing their lives in this pandemic. The Covid-19 virus is the cause of so many people dying, and my grandparents are not far from Wuhan, the city where it all began. My father would have loved to have taken me to the river and baptized me as a Christian.'

Tears began to pour down Song-Wei's face as she thought about her family. Mrs Lacey held out her arms and hugged her and allowed her to cry for as long as she needed. Her emotions had been hidden for far too long. While she was crying, an idea came to Mrs Lacey. She thought she would search on a social media channel and see if the Chinese church in London were streaming a video service. Maybe it would help Song-Wei to hear something in her own language and join with other Chinese Christians.

When she was calmer, as had now become their custom, the three of them closed their eyes and Song-Wei prayed for Will and her own family in Africa and China. She had no idea that Grandpa Lee was also fighting for his life in hospital in China.

– Chapter ten –

Somerset

During the school holidays, the girls had still kept much of their daily routine, and Annelise now spent a lot of the time in the kitchen cooking. She loved baking cakes, and everyone loved eating them! Her self-confidence grew as she discovered that she had a talent and was not useless at all. Her mum encouraged her and found a video of the life story of the famous British cook, Mary Berry. Annelise was amazed to learn that she had been brought up in Bath and struggled at school until she found she loved cooking! The video inspired her to practice her cookery skills and she decided maybe she did know what she would like to do when she left school, after all!

Bill Hodges, the elderly gardener who was now 'furloughed' (not allowed to work but retained with 80% of his salary paid by the government), had begged the girls to look after some of his favourite plants in the greenhouse. Song-Wei took charge of them, as Annelise was now doing so much of the kitchen work. She loved plants but did not know how to tend all of them. Everyone had expected, when the lockdown had been imposed, that it would all be over by Easter, but as the numbers of infections kept increasing throughout April, they realized this was not going to happen.

'Do you know where Mr Hodges lives?' Song-Wei asked Annelise one morning.

'Yes, he lives in a cottage down in the High Street,' Annelise told her. 'I'll show you next time we go to the shop. Why do you want to know?'

'I thought if I could knock on his door, I could talk to him for a bit and ask him about the plants. I'll make sure that I socially distance and wear a mask.'

'That's a cool idea. I'll get mum to phone him. I'm sure he'll be delighted,' her friend answered.

The next day, the girls set out to the village shop. The weather was exceptionally mild for April, so they decided to walk. Annelise pointed out Mr Hodges' house to Song-Wei, and she went to get some shopping while Song-Wei knocked on his door.

Mr Hodges was delighted to see her, and she spent a long time at the doorstep talking with him about the garden and particularly the greenhouse plants. She realized as she talked to the elderly man that he seemed very lonely. His wife had died some years before and their two children lived many miles from Higher Summerfield, unable to visit now due to the lockdown rules.

'They do phone me every weekend to make sure I'm ok, but I only have an old-fashioned phone, not one of those fancy mobile ones where you can see people as well as talk to them. They wanted to buy me one for Christmas, but I told them not to bother. It's too fancy for me; you can't teach an old dog new tricks.'

'Pardon?' said Song-Wei, mystified as to what he meant. Then Mr Hodges realized he had used a saying which she might not understand and gave a hearty laugh, telling her what he meant.

They both dissolved into giggles, and it took a bit of time for them to get back to talking about plants.

'You have done me good young lady; I haven't laughed like that for weeks. Please come and see me again. I might be shut up in this house for months,' he said.

'I will, and I can always bring you shopping if you need it. Just ring Mrs Lacey and she'll tell me what you need.'

'Would you really do that for me?' he answered in surprise. 'That would be very kind.'

When Song-Wei arrived back at Barrow House, she told Mrs Lacey and Annelise all about her chat with Mr Hodges and how lonely he was and needed help with shopping.

'I have an idea,' said Annelise. 'Why don't we make a little notice and deliver one to all the houses in the village, to ask if anyone would help with shopping or fetching medicines and things like that?'

'That's a brilliant idea,' her mum said. 'Let me think how best we can organise it.'

Mrs Lacey discussed the idea with a couple of her friends in the village who were willing to help. She was happy to be the hub organizer and added the idea of adults taking people to the doctor or hospital for routine appointments. The girls designed a small leaflet on the computer, including graphics, while Mrs Lacey ordered a supply of face masks and visors, to keep everyone safe. They decided to call the scheme, 'Helping Hands', and, once they had printed off the leaflets, the girls cycled around the village putting them in every letterbox. Almost two thousand people lived in Higher Summerfield, and many residents were elderly and living alone.

The scheme proved both popular and a lifeline for some of the village residents. Annelise and Song-Wei were able to deliver food parcels to some elderly residents, all of whom were known to the Lacey family, while other young and healthy villagers volunteered to collect prescriptions and drive people to appointments as well as taking shopping to other villagers. The local paper heard about the scheme and asked for an interview with the girls, since it had been their idea. They published a good article, which then led to a socially distanced interview on the local television news. Song-Wei and Annelise were both quite shy, feeling they had done what anyone would have done— just found a way to help their neighbours through a crisis.

They were pleased, though, when they heard that other villages were taking up the scheme and that a food bank had been organised in the church hall to help some of the people who had lost their jobs and could not feed their families.

The summer term started and school lessons were once again reinstated. One morning, in an online class with the Philosophy and Belief teacher, they were all discussing how the pandemic was affecting the places where they lived and how they could help, so the girls told her about the scheme. She was delighted to hear the way in which they were making a difference and how a small idea had grown into something big and useful.

They discussed the way people were clapping each Thursday evening, outside their houses at eight, to honour and say thank you to the frontline key workers. The Lacey household did that, too, even though their house had no close neighbours. It had become a regular event in their week, and they thought of Isobel, Will and Dr Lacey especially, but were grateful for the refuse collectors and the postman and even the boy who delivered the local paper each week.

One day, in early May, good news came to them about Will. He was at last able to breathe on his own and although recovery could take weeks, it was a positive step forward. That evening Annelise and Mrs Lacey joined Song-Wei at their prayer time, speaking for the first time out loud to God to say thank you.

Song-Wei still had no news from her family in China or Africa, and what seemed even more strange was that she had not heard from her guardian, Aunt Wong-Jong. She phoned, texted and wrote letters but had no answer. She thought that perhaps she was still in lockdown in Hong Kong. A highlight of her week was to watch online services from the Chinese church in London. Just to hear her own language spoken and hear stories of how God was looking after people in China and that the pandemic seemed to be easing, was very comforting.

It continued warm and dry for most of the month of May, so the girls were able to be out and about in the afternoons and evenings. Song-Wei became more and more involved with the garden, learning a lot from Mr Hodges as she now visited him several times a week. He learnt from her, too, as she told him about the herbs which were used by her family to help sick people.

'I think I might like to study horticulture at university,' she told him, one day. The old man smiled. He had taken to sitting on a garden bench outside his front door while he talked to Song-Wei.

'We were just jobbing gardeners when I was a boy,' he told her. 'I was lucky to get a job as a garden boy up at the big house and then stay there all my working life. I was head gardener at one time, but that was when they still had a servant or two, long before the Laceys came. It still belonged to the lord of the manor.'

'What's a "lord of the manor"?' she asked Mr Hodges. 'I don't understand.'

Mr Hodges explained the way the feudal system in England had developed and continued to some extent right into the twentieth century, and how the 'lord of the manor' had been held in great respect by the people living on the estate he owned and those who worked for him. It was strange to Song-Wei who was used to a totalitarian government, where everyone was supposed to be equal. Somehow the two of them discussed the pros and cons, even though Mr Hodges spoke in a broad Somerset accent and Song-Wei in slightly broken English. A deep bond of affection was growing between them and, to Song-Wei, he became another grandfather.

One afternoon Annelise and Song-Wei were surprised to see Mrs Lacey arrive in the old nursery carrying a sewing machine.

'This was your granny's sewing machine,' she told Annelise. 'It's about fifty years old and I think I can remember how to use it. When Isobel and Will were small and your dad just a junior doctor, we had little money to live on, so my mother gave this to me. She thought it would help if I made their clothes. I tried but was never much good at it. However, now there is a real need to try again. It seems that this virus is not going away any time soon, so people may be asked to wear masks in public places all the time. I thought we could learn to make some. I've downloaded a pattern from the internet and printed off some copies. I decided we could start by using this spare sheet, and Maggie had some elastic in the shop.

'Let's see how we get on, and if we can work out how to make them, we'll make enough for all the people who are shut in and shielding in the village.'

'Oh Mum,' groaned Annelise. 'I'm useless at sewing. Mrs Brown, our textile teacher, won't even let me near the machines. I think she is sure I will break them!'

Mrs Lacey laughed. 'You and I are so alike! I never passed a needlework exam. My mum tried to teach me and gave up in desperation!'

'Yes, but you are clever, and I'm useless at everything,' said Annelise sadly.

'Don't ever say that,' her Mum said. 'We all have different gifts, and we are all special. You have discovered cooking and baking skills. You are amazing! Sometimes we need to be pushed into a corner before we find out what we can do. Granny tells me it was like that growing up in the war. People had no choice. They had to learn new skills or starve, or let the nation be taken over by the enemy. In a way, we are in a war now. Our enemy is the Covid-19 virus. You can see how the community has begun to pull together and help each other. Neighbours are talking to each other, checking up that everyone is safe and well. It was like that in the war. If you had something, say lots of fruit in the garden, then you shared it with your family and neighbours. That was how the country survived. We will survive this virus, but we need to help each other. I am so proud of you girls and your 'Helping Hands' scheme—and now it's spreading all over the county.

'So, this is our next challenge. First, we'll cut out the patterns and measure the pieces of elastic. I'll thread up the machine—if I can remember how. If not, I'll message Granny; she will remember.'

'I think I can thread the machine,' Song-Wei said. 'It looks a bit like the one Grandma Lee has. I love the idea of helping the community.'

It was a shaky start, but they soon got the hang of making masks, and managed two each by the end of the afternoon. All three were proud of their achievements.

'We are so busy these days with all our activities, that I even forget to look on social media to see what my friends are up to and I never play games on my phone now,' laughed Annelise.

'I think that's probably a good thing for all of us; less screen time and more social activity,' her Mum commented. 'Anyway, when we feel confident about sewing these masks, we have an even bigger challenge. Dad has said they are desperate for scrubs to wear in the hospital and so I thought I'd try to source a pattern and we could try those.'

'Wow!' said Annelise, her eyes growing wide. 'You mean we'll make real things for people to wear? That would be so cool and to be able to help Dad and Will would be amazing!'

'We'll go on slowly with making masks until we are confident and then we'll see what we can do.'

– CHAPTER ELEVEN –

Somerset

Although Annelise and Song-Wei missed their dorm-mates and other school friends, they kept happy and busy as the weeks continued to pass. They posted their achievements from time to time on social media for their friends to see and got lots of good comments on their masks and Annelise's baking. At times, they felt annoyed by the restrictions. As Annelise once put it, 'they were like birds in a cage who were occasionally let out'.

Song-Wei was so grateful to be with Annelise. They rarely argued and had a lot of fun together.

'This lockdown time is so strange,' remarked Annelise at lunch one day. 'So many people have been shut up like prisoners in their own homes. We are sort of semi-prisoners, while others are trapped in their own countries and not allowed to travel anywhere. It's kind of weird. We are all used to being free to do what we want to do and go where we like and now we can't anymore.'

'In the seventeenth century, one of the English poets wrote these words,' answered her mum. 'I can't remember all the poem, but these two lines have stuck in my mind since schooldays: "Stone walls do not a prison make, nor iron bars a cage". I have often thought about that when I have been working with some of my clients. They are in prisons of worry, fear or believing things in their minds which are not true. Their lives are then limited because these thoughts have imprisoned them. It happens so easily. People can be in an actual prison, but still be free in their hearts and minds.'

The girls were quiet for a minute or two while they thought about this. Then Annelise suddenly smiled. 'That's like me,' she said. 'I have always thought that I was useless at everything; not clever like you and dad, Will and Isobel. I thought I must be a great disappointment to you, but since we've been in lockdown, I have found out I can cook and love doing it. I do feel different inside because I know I am good at something.'

'Sweetheart, you are amazing just being you and we love you for who you are. You have never been a disappointment to us, just a great joy. I had several miscarriages both before you were born and afterwards; I wanted two more children, but you were the only one given to us, and you are all the more precious because of that,' answered her Mum.

'Oh Mum, thank you. That's so cool of you to tell me that. I never knew. I thought perhaps I was an 'accident', and you hadn't planned to have me and maybe I was a nuisance as you had a good career.'

'Nothing could be further from the truth,' declared her Mum, giving her daughter a huge hug. 'Those were wrong thoughts imprisoning you. I'm glad we've got that sorted out!'

That evening Isobel was able to get a connection from The Gambia to video call the family. It was exciting because she had some news. The Covid-19 virus was well contained in the country, but she was staying on as she enjoyed the work and research in which she was involved. But there was another reason she did not want to return to England just yet. She had made a friendship, which was growing into something deeper with a young doctor from the United States who was also working in the same hospital. She was explaining this to her mother and Annelise, when Tanner came to the screen and introduced himself.

'Wow! he's so cool!' commented Annelise after the video call was finished. 'Trust Izzie to find a dishy boyfriend!'

Her mother laughed. 'It's a good job they are thousands of miles away, or you might be swooning after Tanner, too. You have too much schoolwork to do before you start thinking about boyfriends.'

It was fantastic to know that Isobel was well and happy, and Annelise sent text messages to both Will and her dad, just in case they had not yet heard the news.

The following evening there was more news, but this time it was not so good. They had just finished supper, a yummy beef casserole cooked by Annelise, when the phone rang. Annelise ran to answer it. 'It's probably a client who needs medicines collected or shopping done,' she said cheerfully to her Mum. Annelise had become good at taking and recording messages since they had started the 'Helping Hands' scheme. Song-Wei did not like to answer the phone as her English was not so good and she still spoke with an accent. Some of the older people were not able to understand her very well and she found the Somerset accent hard, although she had become used to listening to Mr. Hodges.

'Good evening, Barrow House,' Annelise said, as she lifted the receiver.

'Good evening, Annelise. This is Miss Boston. Please could I speak with your mother?'

'Yes, certainly, Miss Boston. I'll take the phone to her.'

Both girls wondered what their head teacher wanted to say. Maybe school would restart sooner than they thought, or perhaps they could not go back this term?

After about half an hour, Mrs Lacey appeared in the kitchen.

'I've had a long talk with Miss Boston and now need to have a wee chat to Song-Wei. Thanks for clearing up the supper things,' she said, looking around the kitchen. 'Annelise, would you mind taking Goldie out for his evening walk around the garden, while we have a chat in the snug?'

Song-Wei's heart went so cold, it felt like a stone in her chest. Had something happened to her family? One look at her aunt's face told her something was wrong. She began to shake a little, and her fears became greater as Mrs Lacey put her arms around her and gave her a hug.

Outside, Annelise was feeling upset as well. She could see her Mum was troubled and the news must be serious for her to be sent to take Goldie for a walk. As she walked, tears sprang into her eyes and a lump of apprehension came in her throat. Was there bad news for her friend, who had become like a sister to her? She decided to talk to God—it had helped when Will was so sick. So, as she walked around the large garden, she asked God to help Song-Wei, whatever news she had to hear.

'Song-Wei, sweetheart, I have sad news to tell you,' Mrs Lacey began. As far as we know, your family are ok—at least, this news is not from China or Congo. It's from Hong Kong. Your dear guardian, Wong-Jong, caught Covid-19 and became extremely sick, and sadly, has passed away. It has taken some time for the news to come to England to inform one of her friends, who has just let Miss Boston know.

'I am so sorry, dear. I know you were very close to her, and she was "family" to you in this country.'

Song-Wei was sobbing, trying to take in the news and the fact that she would never see Aunt Wong-Jong again, and never be able to say 'goodbye' to her.

Over the next few days and nights, Song-Wei found it difficult to sleep after hearing this news and the implications of her position began to sink in. Her guardian had not only given her a home in London but had kept in touch with what was happening to her parents and grandparents. Money was sent to her guardian's Hong Kong bank account to pay her school fees, buy her uniform and other needs. Now she realized that she was alone in a foreign country with no means of support. It dawned on her that, although she had been invited to stay with Annelise, it was expected that it would only be for a short time, but already it was stretching from weeks to months, and she had no money to give her hosts for her food and lodging.

What would happen to her if she could no longer attend St. Catherine's school? Song-Wei thought she might have to become a refugee, for she had no way to return to China.

Song-Wei did not want to be a nuisance or a burden to her lovely new friends, but she was frightened about her future.

In the days which followed she tried to be cheerful and enjoy her life, but nothing was the same as before. She felt as if she were wearing a huge backpack full of worries that she could not take off.

Mrs Lacey began to be concerned. Song-Wei was withdrawing into her own little world and not eating very well. She only took tiny portions of food, even when it was a Chinese evening and she had cooked the meal.

'Annelise,' her Mum asked, one evening when Song-Wei had gone to her bedroom instead of staying in the snug and watching a DVD as they sometimes did. 'Do you think Song-Wei is ok? She seems so quiet and worried these days. I think it may be more than the loss of her guardian, sad though that is.'

'I don't know, Mum,' Annelise answered. 'She talks about the lessons we are doing, sometimes about the garden and the greenhouse, and she seems ok on the outside, but it's as if the spark has gone out on the inside.'

'She's been teaching us how to pray. Maybe we should pray together for her?' suggested her mum.

Annelise looked at her mum in surprise and then nodded. 'Yep, that's a good idea.'

Mother and daughter were a little shy and not exactly comfortable about praying together, but they held hands, and both said a short prayer asking God to help Song-Wei through her difficulties.

Meanwhile, in her bedroom, Song-Wei had also been trying to pray, but God seemed far away. She had never really felt like this before, even when she first arrived in London and everything had been so strange, and she felt homesick. Now she felt abandoned—as if God was not hearing her prayers and had gone away. She opened her Bible randomly, and she found that she was looking at a verse in the book of Hebrews.

'I will never leave you nor forsake you,' she read from chapter 13 and verse 5 (ESV). All the rest of the words around seemed a blur, but these few words stood out and almost shouted at her.

'Is this true, Father God?' she whispered. 'Then I'm sorry that I doubted you. Please help me.'

Then into her mind came a song which she used to sing in church in China.

> The Lord is above me, below me, around me, he walks beside me, every day of my life.
> He feeds the hungry, a friend to the lonely, he heals the sick ones and strengthens the weak.
> The Lord is a strong tower which can never be shaken, his children run into it and always are safe.

It seemed to Song-Wei, as she quietly sung these words to herself, that at last the backpack was slipping off a little and she could lie down and sleep. She slept soundly that night, without worrying or having bad dreams.

– CHAPTER TWELVE –

Somerset

The next day Song-Wei woke refreshed and although the worries and fears were still there, they did not feel so heavy.

It was a very wet day. The weather had been amazingly good throughout March, April and much of May—but this day it had changed. Song-Wei knew that the garden needed the rain and that the farmers had been praying for it, but since it was a Saturday, she wondered how she and Annelise would occupy themselves.

Mrs Lacey had already thought about that and at breakfast asked the girls to help her with some spring-cleaning. Annelise groaned. 'Do we have to?' she asked.

'No, but it would help me a lot if you did,' commented her mum. Song-Wei wanted to do all she could to help as she felt she was a burden on the family.

'I'll help,' she said, with a smile, 'but I must do my violin practice first. I promised my teacher I would practice every day. Is that OK?'

'Well, I'll do the prep for our evening meal, then I'll help, too.' Annelise decided.

They were asked to clean and tidy the wardrobes and chests of drawers in their bedrooms and then, after a break, to tackle the nursery room, especially the cupboards and bookcases.

Song-Wei found herself singing as she worked. Her room was the easiest to clean as she did not have many things. Once she had finished cleaning and tidying the inside of the wardrobe, she looked at the outside. It was large and made from a dark wood, beautifully carved with flowers, birds, and fruits. She knew it must be old. Maybe it had been in the house for a few hundred years. It certainly looked as if it belonged there. She decided to polish it and climbed on a chair to reach the highest carvings. Admiring them, she polished each piece lovingly. One rose carving, when she polished it, seemed to turn slightly in her hand. Then it made a weird noise which scared her so much that she fell off the chair with a scream. Annelise came rushing in from her room next door.

'What's happened?' she asked. 'Are you hurt?' Song-Wei was still on the floor, holding her ankle.

'I was polishing the carvings on the wardrobe, when one bit moved and made such a weird noise that it scared me and I fell off the chair. My ankle hurts. I landed heavily on it,' she answered.

'Don't move. I'll go and fetch Mum,' Annelise said, rushing out of the door and downstairs to find her mother, who was cleaning the pantry.

Minutes later, Mrs Lacey looked at Song-Wei's ankle and thought that it was sprained, so put on a bandage to support it. Song-Wei's colour had returned, and she was able to stand, even though it still hurt a lot.

'What were you doing standing on a chair?' Mrs Lacey asked her. So, she told the story once again and everyone looked up at the wardrobe.

'Wow, it looks as if it has a secret drawer. How cool is that?' said Annelise. 'Did you know about that, Mum?' she asked.

'I had no idea,' she answered. 'When we bought this house it included a lot of the furniture, too. The people who sold it to us told us that they had bought it complete with the furniture, which they thought had been installed when the house was built. Let me get a step ladder. That will be safer than standing on a chair.'

Inside the drawer they discovered a couple of old letters and a jewellery box, which Mrs Lacey took out and laid on Song-Wei's bed.

The girls looked at each other in excitement. 'Have we found some treasure?' Annelise asked.

The box was closed with a clasp which was old and fragile, so Mrs Lacey very gently prised it open, trying not to force it. When she lifted the lid, the three of them gasped in surprise.

Inside they found a beautiful necklace, set with stones; a bracelet which matched; and a ring.

'My guess is that these jewels are diamonds, rubies and sapphires,' Mrs Lacey told the girls.

'What a discovery! Let's take them downstairs with the letters. We'll have a break and look to see if there is any clue as to whose they were.'

The girls were bubbling with excitement and it made Song-Wei think it was well worth spraining her ankle! Annelise helped her hobble down the stairs and into the snug.

'First of all, I'm going to ring the cottage hospital to see if they will check your ankle and do an x-ray,' Mrs Lacey told Song-Wei. 'My guess is that those jewels have been hidden for many years so they can wait just a little longer while we sort out your ankle.'

Mrs Lacey was asked to take Song-Wei to the cottage hospital in the nearby small town. Because of the pandemic, Annelise had to stay behind, so reluctantly she promised to finish the spring clean of her bedroom and then prepare lunch. Her Mum locked the find in the safe, because she sensed they might prove to be valuable.

Waiting for the x-ray at the hospital gave Mrs Lacey an opportunity to chat to Song-Wei. She was conscious that she still seemed troubled about the death of her guardian and wanted to see if she could help.

'We love having you stay with us, Song-Wei,' she said, 'and so glad you weren't sent to a children's home. I know you must be feeling devastated to hear about Auntie Wong-Jong, but I want you to know that we are here for you and if we can help in any way, we will.'

Maybe it was the shock of falling off the chair and the pain in her ankle, but suddenly Song-Wei felt tired and weepy. A big tear dripped down her face, quickly followed by another one. She tried to hold them back, but just was not able to.

'You have been so kind to me but, now I have lost Auntie Wong-Jong, I realize I am on my own, a refugee in this country. Auntie helped pay my school fees and was in contact with my family in China, so that I knew what was happening to my parents and grandparents. She paid for my keep in the holidays and bought my uniform and things I needed, even paying for my violin lessons. Now she has gone, I am frightened and have no money. How can I go back to school? I have nowhere to go, no money and am unable to go home to China. I guess I will be put into a children's home after all and just be a burden to your country. I know that Jesus is with me and has promised He will never leave me, but I still feel so alone.'

Song-Wei did not mean to let Mrs Lacey or Annelise know how she felt, but somehow it just spilled out of her mouth and, in a way, she was glad she had shared her problem.

Mrs Lacey put her arm around Song-Wei and tried to comfort her.

'Just now we are all facing an uncertain future, but for the present time, however long lockdown may last, you are welcome in our home as our guest. When school starts again, we will talk with Miss Boston about your future. There are things called bursaries, which pay the fees of good students when their families cannot afford the money. I'll investigate it all for you and, if you are able to stay at St. Catherine's, then our home will be your home in the holidays for as long as you need one. You have been a blessing in our home, and we all love you very much, so dry your tears because I'm sure that the doctor will call you soon.'

As Song-Wei listened to Mrs Lacey, it was as if the backpack full worries had fallen off forever. God had heard her prayer; this kind family, whom she loved, would take care of her and help her.

'Thank you, Aunt Julia,' she said. 'I don't know how to say thank you. I have been so worried about the future. I love you, too. You are so kind to me!'

By the time she was back at Barrow House, her ankle bandaged, and a crutch to use until the pain was gone, Song-Wei was smiling again, and excited to see the treasure they had found.

– CHAPTER THIRTEEN –

Somerset

The treasure looked amazing. That evening, Mrs Lacey took it from the safe and they all looked at it carefully. None of them knew anything about antique jewellery, but in Bath there were many antique shops and jewellers who would do a valuation.

'My guess is that we will have to wait until lockdown is over and all the shops are allowed to reopen before we can find out much about the value of these jewels,' Mrs Lacey told the girls. 'I'll photograph them and lock them in the safe for the time being. It would be best not to tell all your friends about the find until we know more. Should it reach the local paper, then we might find someone trying to break in to steal or making up some false story claiming them. We can talk to Dad and show him when he comes home next time.'

'Look Mum,' exclaimed Annelise. 'There's some writing inside the bracelet—it's very tiny. I'm going to find my magnifying glass and try to read what it says. It might give us some clues.'

Annelise ran to her room and back at top speed and then looked at the inscription again.

'I can read it,' she said in delight. 'Elspeth McDougal-Baker = Francis Stephen Wicks June 22nd, 1731.'

'Wow! Isn't that just so cool! Maybe it was a wedding gift?' she added.

'The equals sign is used in family trees to indicate marriage,' her Mum agreed. 'Write down the two names and we'll do some investigating. It should be interesting to see if we can find out more. We may have to wait until the end of this lockdown for the treasure to be valued. However, we might discover something about the family before then if we search the internet.'

'We have the letters we can read,' said Song-Wei. 'They might give us more clues.'

'It's like being detectives,' Annelise said. 'We have to piece the bits of information together and see what we can deduce.'

'I think all of us will have fun working on this mystery,' her mum added, 'but we must be careful with the old letters, as they will be fragile. I'll see if I can find some old cotton gloves for us to wear. I think Grandma may have some she could send us. She never throws anything away, always thinking it might come in useful one day. She used to wear cotton gloves when she was young. I've no doubt she'll be delighted to help.'

The girls thought it was so cool to have something new and exciting to think about and a mystery to try and solve. Lockdown had been in place for three months and they all needed a new focus, especially since the fine weather had developed into a different pattern, with lots of showers as well as sunshine.

The government gave an update every afternoon concerning the number of new cases of the virus and the number of deaths recorded. It all sounded so depressing and sad. News on the television from China was sparse, but it did seem that a second wave was attacking the area of Wuhan, the city where the pandemic seemed to have begun, which was not far from Song-Wei's hometown.

Now, in the UK, there were plans for a 'track and trace' system, which would allow people a little more freedom to move around. The messages seemed very confusing and people were not sure quite what they could or could not do. Certainly, schools were not reopening, and the national GCSE, BTEC and A level examinations had been cancelled. Annelise and Song-Wei were glad they were not taking any external exams, although Song-Wei was due to take Grade 5 violin. She enjoyed playing it and practised every day up in the old nursery.

Over the next few days, Annelise and Song-Wei settled down to try to find out the history of Barrow House, using the search engine on their laptops and hoping to find out who the people were whose names were engraved on the bracelet. They learnt that Barrow house had been built in 1720 for a family who were landowners in the area both of Higher Summerfield and Combe Down, a village just outside Bath, where they owned a sheep farm. They discovered that the wool industry was important at that time of the country's history and the wool from the Combe Down farm was sent to Bradford-Upon-Avon in nearby Wiltshire, to be processed in the mills there. It was highly prized wool and a good source of income for the family who were obviously connected to Elspeth, to whom the jewellery had belonged, because their surname was McDougal.

'Aunt Julia, may I ask Mr Hodges if he knows anything about the history of the house or the inhabitants? I won't tell him about the treasure we have found,' asked Song-Wei. 'He seems to know a lot about the village and this area.'

'Yes, certainly—though I doubt that he would know anything so far back,' Mrs Lacey replied.

'Thank you, that's cool. I was planning to go and see him this afternoon, but I'm not sure I can walk that far, and I might wobble too much on my bike, but I'll visit as soon as I can.'

'I can drop you at his cottage, Mrs Lacey replied. 'I need to go to Paulton and take things to the food bank there and have prescriptions to collect and deliver around the village. I'll call for you on my way back. What are you going to do, Annelise?'

'Can you take me to the shop, please? Maggie has ordered some potato flour for me. I want to try out a new cake recipe for tonight's dessert. It's our English evening so I will be glad to have the kitchen to myself.'

'You really love cooking, don't you?' said her mum. 'I'm glad you have found something you enjoy, and it helps me so much, even if it doesn't help my waistline!'

Mr Hodges was delighted to see Song-Wei. He looked forward to her visits and, when he heard about her ankle, he was upset and thought he might not see her for a while.

'I want to teach you how to pinch out the top of the tomato plants,' he said. 'I guess they are growing nicely now.'

'Oh yes please,' she replied, showing him a photo on her phone. Mr Hodges looked at the picture, then pointed out the leaves which needed to be removed.

'You are proving to be a splendid gardener,' he praised her. 'I find it hard to believe that you have lived all your life in a flat which didn't even have a balcony. You are a natural at it. Don't stop when you start back to school. Do they allow you to garden in your school?'

'I don't know, but there are lovely gardens and I'm going to ask, if I can still go back there,' she answered, her voice wobbling a little with emotion at the thought of what could happen. Then she explained to Mr Hodges a little about the uncertainty of her future.

'Aunt Julia has told me not to worry, and that I have a home with them for now, and I know that God will take care of me, but it's hard not to worry at all,' she told the old man.

'They are a good family, and you are right to trust in God. He has taken care of me and my family for many years. Did I ever tell you that my great grandfather was once the vicar of the church here?'

'No, you didn't. That's so cool. My father is a pastor of a small church—or was until he was sent to work in the Congo—but it isn't easy to be a pastor in our country and he doesn't get paid for his work. He has another job in management and is overseeing the construction of a hospital just now.' Song-Wei took a deep breath, not really wanting to talk about her fears for her parents working in a remote tropical forest.

'I'm interested in the history of this village and Barrow House. We have been finding out on the internet the date it was built and the first owners. Do you know any history as back as far as 1720?' Song-Wei asked.

'Not really,' answered Mr Hodges, with a twinkle in his eye. 'I'm not quite that old!' he chuckled to himself, 'but, come to think of it, I do have a book somewhere. My great grandfather, the vicar, wrote a history of the village and the area around here. It used to be a coal mining area—you wouldn't think that now with all this lovely countryside around us. If you like, I'll go and see if I can find it for you? It might help you to find out more.'

Mr Hodges disappeared into his cottage and Song-Wei sat outside in the sunshine, thanking God for all the lovely countryside she could see, and for Mr Hodges and all he had taught her about plants and growing them.

A few minutes later, he reappeared, waving a small book in his hand. 'I found it!' he said, smiling broadly. 'You can keep it for as long as you like, but when you have finished with it, I'd like it back, seeing it was written by my ancestors.'

'I will take care of it. Thank you so much.' replied Song-Wei, taking the book carefully from him.

A few minutes later, Mrs Lacey appeared. She came up the garden path holding a little box of biscuits.

'Here's a treat for you, Bill,' she said. 'I'm glad to see you so fit and well. Thank you for teaching Song-Wei so much. She is a great help looking after the greenhouse and some of the garden. She has come like a gift from God to our family at this time. I don't know how we would have managed without her.'

'Nor me,' replied Mr. Hodges. 'I look forward to her visits so much. She keeps me cheerful and gives me something to look forward to each week. I'm glad to know the garden is doing well.'

Song-Wei blushed with all the praise. She felt she did not deserve any of it, but it did make her feel loved and glad she was not a burden to Annelise's family.

– CHAPTER FOURTEEN –

China, 2020

At the hospital in China, after several very hectic weeks due to the high numbers of patients sick with the Covid-19 virus, infection rates at last began to slow down. There were less new admissions of seriously ill patients and less deaths. The staff had worked so hard that they were exhausted. Grandpa Lee had begun to recover but was still weak and unable to walk any distance. His wife was worried because he looked pale and was tired after even the smallest exertion. She decided she should stop her work as a cook, and they should return to their apartment. She was determined to nurse him back to full health before Song-Wei's parents returned home from the Congo.

Each Saturday, Grandma Lee wrote a long letter to Lydia and John. She posted it to the headquarters of the construction firm and knew it would eventually arrive some weeks later, when a plane or truck went to the village in the forest.

One day, Grandma Lee received a message which had taken weeks to reach her from Hong Kong and she learnt of the sad death Wong-Jong. It was such a shock to hear that she had died from the Covid-19 virus while visiting Hong Kong. This increased her concerns even more—what would happen to Song-Wei now, living alone in a foreign country without support? Grandma Lee's family were now spread all over the world and she felt so sad at not being able to help them, but she sat down and wrote a letter at once to her daughter to tell her about the sad news, in case she had not yet heard it. She had no idea what else she could do except ask God to take care of her precious granddaughter. The concern hung over her like a dark cloud and when she visited Grandpa Lee, her face was downcast.

'Whatever is the matter?' he asked her. 'Don't try to protect me if you have bad news. I am getting better and we will face whatever it is together.'

So, Grandma Lee shared the letter she had just received. 'I don't know what to do,' she confessed. 'I feel so helpless!'

'Let's recite Psalm 27 together,' Grandpa Lee suggested. How glad they were that they had memorized some of the Psalms in the Bible when they were young. That Psalm had always brought them comfort, but this time, as they reached the end and said the words,

'I am still confident of this: I will see the goodness of the Lord in the land of the living.

Wait for the Lord; be strong and take heart and wait for the Lord' (vv. 13–14), they came with fresh meaning to them. It was as if the Lord was whispering, 'Wait, be strong and take heart— for all will be well.'

One morning, a week later, Grandma Lee went to the administrator's office to give in her notice.

'Good morning, Mrs Lee. What can I do for you?' she was asked.

'I think that I can no longer work here as a cook,' she answered. 'My husband has been sick with the Covid-19 disease and is still very weak. He will not be able to return to work as a porter, so I wish to leave and go home to take care of him.'

The administrator was a kindly older man. He looked at Grandma Lee and smiled.

'You have been a blessing to us, and your roast chicken is now a legend around the hospital. Your husband, too, was a good porter and worked hard and cheerfully. We thank you for what you have done to help us through this difficult time. I fear that Mr Lee possibly has what is now being called, 'Long Covid', and may have a long battle ahead to get fit and well. We know so little about this disease that is spreading throughout the world.

'Please may I ask you to stay with us for one more week? We will keep your husband on the ward until then. That will give me time to recruit another cook—though it won't be easy.'

As Grandma Lee left his office, she felt peace filling her. She knew that God would take care of her and her husband, and the rest of the family, even though they were miles apart and not able to be in regular contact with each other.

One week later, Grandma Lee went back to the administrator and he asked her to sit down.

'I have a suggestion to put to you,' he said. 'It is just that: a suggestion, an alternative plan.

I have been told that your daughter and son-in-law are serving our country, by working in the Democratic Republic of the Congo, building a hospital, and so, for the time being, cannot look after you.

'If you would like it, we have a bungalow in our hospital grounds which could become your home until your family return. It is fully furnished so you would only need to bring your personal items from your apartment. Your husband would have no stairs to worry about, and we can supply a hospital bed and a wheelchair for him, which would make nursing easier for you. When Mr Lee becomes stronger, you will always be welcome to work once again in the kitchen, should you so wish.'

Grandma Lee was glad she was sitting down! What had they done to deserve such kindness?

'This is so unexpected and so kind,' she stammered. 'I do not know how to thank you.'

'This is about us wanting to thank and honour you,' the administrator replied. 'You did not have to come in your old age and work in such a dangerous environment and for no pay, but you came because you have a heart of love for your country and people. I know, too, that you are Christians and love God, and I admire you for your faith. There is one more thing,' he added, bringing from behind his desk a large bouquet of flowers and handing them to Grandma Lee.

'Oh, they are so beautiful!' she exclaimed, burying her nose in the flowers and trying not to cry. 'Thank you so much, for everything.'

He rang a bell and in walked a young lady. 'Please take these keys and show Mrs Lee the bungalow, and then if she is happy to live in the bungalow, we will make arrangements for the move.'

'One more thing, Mrs Lee,' he said with a twinkle in his eye. 'Make your chicken dish once more for us all before you finally leave the kitchen!'

Grandma Lee was overwhelmed by the kindness and appreciation she was shown. In her heart she thanked God. She had hoped that, by volunteering to help, it would bless her country and make a difference, but she had not expected that anyone would notice her. She was just a kitchen helper, and her husband a porter. They were not important like the doctors and nurses, but the administrator had seen the love of Jesus through them helping, and that was reward enough!

– CHAPTER FIFTEEN –

Congo

Far away, in the Ituri forest, Lydia had been thinking. Did God really want her and John to stay in the Congo? What about Song-Wei? What about her parents? She worried about them all. She knew she needed to decide soon, and asked God to make it clear if they were to stay in Africa. The hospital was almost completed and ready for patients. Some Congolese medical staff had been recruited from a teaching hospital near the town of Bunia, called Nyankunde. The forest hospital was quite small, so would not need too many staff—at least to begin with. The maternity block was ready to admit patients, and Lydia had been trained in midwifery as well as general nursing, so could begin work soon. If only she knew what the right thing to do would be.

'Hodi', called a voice at her door (may I enter?).

'Karibu', Lydia answered (welcome, come in).

A young girl came into the kitchen, the whites of her eyes red from crying. She was dirty and wearing a dress which was torn, and she knelt on the floor, looking at Lydia with beseeching eyes.

'Mama, kuja, kuja', she begged, reaching out and taking Lydia's hand when she reached out to touch her.

Lydia knew 'kuja' meant 'come', so she followed the little girl through the village and to a track which led her deep into the forest. The trees around were so tall and majestic, and underneath them the ground was covered with lush ferns. There were flashes of colour from beautiful orchids growing in the trees. The girl led her to what seemed to be a deserted Pygmy village and she entered one of the huts. It was a stick and straw hut with a dirt floor. Lydia bent down to enter the dwelling, her eyes struggling to adapt to the darkness. On a rush mat lay a very pregnant woman, who looked exhausted and in great pain. Lydia guessed the woman was probably having a difficult labour. The little girl looked terrified as she watched her mother in such great pain, her eyes large and full of tears. Lydia thought quickly about what she should do and prayed silently, asking God to help her. She gently beckoned the little girl to come near and whispered to her in a mixture of poor French and even worse Kingwana, to bring some water and soap.

The little girl must have understood enough for she disappeared from the hut. Lydia gently lifted the cloth which the woman had around her waist and examined the swollen stomach. Then she put her ear near to see if she could hear the baby's heartbeat. Her own heart was beating so loudly that it was hard to concentrate and hear anything, but after a while she thought she could detect a weak, rapid beat. That meant the baby was alive but possibly in distress. As Lydia gently felt all around the stomach, she was sure that the baby was lying across the womb in a wrong position. No wonder the woman was in such pain. If she did not do something very quickly, the mother might rupture her womb and then both she and the baby would die.

Lydia took off the cotton petticoat which she was wearing under her dress and tore it into strips, as there did not seem to be any clean towels or materials in the hut.

She heard a noise and looked up to see the little girl coming in with a plastic bowl and a yellow can of water. The poor child could hardly manage to carry them.

'Asante sana, merci beaucoup', Lydia said, gratefully. When the water, soap and basin were safely on the floor, she took the girl's hand and placed it in her mother's. She showed her how to stroke it gently, thinking it would give comfort to the woman and keep the little girl occupied.

Then she washed her hands as best she could and, kneeling beside the woman, she prayed again for the survival of the mother and baby and for strength to turn the infant. Lydia did an internal examination and found the mother was ready to deliver, so she waited until a contraction had finished, then put her hand into the womb and managed to turn the baby around into the correct position for it to be born. The poor mother was so tired, but when the next contraction arrived, Lydia shouted, 'Push!' and put her hand on her tummy to help show the mother what she wanted her to do. With great relief, Lydia saw the baby's head appearing and was able to deliver him safely.

The baby boy looked pale and did not cry at once, but Lydia wrapped him in a piece of her torn petticoat and gently rubbed him and smacked his bottom. Eventually, he gave a big yell.

The mother was crying with relief and so was Lydia. She gave the baby to the mum while she began to clean up the mess.

She thanked God that she had arrived in time to help and both had survived.

The little girl suddenly ran out of the hut and Lydia did not know whether she could find her way home or should stay where she was. She glanced at her watch and saw it was noon. The girl who helped her in her house should be there preparing food. She needed to get a message to her.

The little girl appeared again, carrying a tin cup with a drink in it and gave it to her mother.

Once again, Lydia beckoned her, not wanting to frighten her, and tried to ask her to go back to the house and get help. With lots of gestures and a few words of various languages, the little girl seemed to understand and ran quickly out of the hut.

Lydia then tidied up as much as she could and wrapped the little boy in another clean piece of cloth. The mother fed him and then tucked him by her side and they both fell asleep.

As Lydia waited for the girl to return, hopefully with her house helper, she prayed for this little family. Then, she was suddenly sure why this had happened. God had shown her how much she was needed here in the Congo. Maternity services were non-existent in much of the forest area and when complications arose, if there was no-one to help, both mother and baby would die.

'I'll stay, Lord,' she prayed, 'but please look after my daughter and my parents while I am so far away from them.' Then she felt a sense of peace and joy as she looked at the sleeping mother and baby and knew God had heard her prayer.

Soon Lydia heard footsteps and in came the little girl with not only the house help, Penina, but also the garden helper, Kimweli.

'When we heard what happened, I thought Kimweli would make a stretcher and we can carry the mother and baby to your house until Bwana comes home. He can then drive her to the big hospital in the town if she needs more care. Shairi can come too, to be near her mother. Her father is on a hunting expedition with others from the tribe. The whole village has moved on to another site, but as her mother was so heavily pregnant, they left her behind in the hut with Shairi to help. She does not know when her father will return, but I am sure he will come to the village to look for his wife when he does.'

'Should we leave a note to say what happened?' Lydia asked.

Penina and Kimweli burst out laughing. 'These people cannot read or write, Madame. Do not worry—he will come for news of his family. News travels through the bush.'

Kimweli made a good stretcher out of bamboo poles tied up with strong twine from a climbing plant. Carefully they lifted the mother on to it and put the baby beside her. Then began the trek through the forest to the village.

Penina was a marvellous help. She put a mattress on the veranda, and they laid the mother there. Then, she heated water and washed the mother properly, while Lydia washed the baby and found a clean towel in which to wrap him. Penina explained to Lydia that she was taking Shairi, the little girl, to her house to give her a shower and find some clothes which might fit her.

'I'll cook beans and rice for an evening meal for them, too. If you can make some hot, sweet chai for the mother, that will be good,' she added.

With everything well organised, the time seemed to fly by. For the first time since their arrival in Congo, Lydia felt completely happy, at peace and useful.

- Chapter sixteen -

Congo

John was surprised when he arrived home from his work to see the mattress with the mother and baby on the veranda! Beside her, on a little wooden stool sat Penina, with Shairi, now looking very pretty in a dress which one of Penina's daughters had outgrown. Lydia heard Penina greet John and rushed out to explain to him all about the day's events.

Speaking in Mandarin, she smiled at her husband, 'I know now that we must stay here and help these people. God has shown that to me today.' He could see how happy Lydia was and that made his heart light.

'I am so glad you feel that way,' he said. 'It is what I feel, too, but I wanted you to feel the same before I spoke with the boss.'

That evening, he drove the mother and baby, along with Lydia, Penina and Shairi and Kimweli, to the forest hospital located in a place called Oicha (pronounced oo-each-ahh). Oicha had once been just a small collection of huts, not big enough to be a village, in a clearing in the forest, but then a missionary doctor built a small clinic to help the forest people. This was so successful and, because there were many people with leprosy, the place had grown and was now the second largest town in the forest region.

Kimweli had begged to go along, and John was relieved, as it was not easy navigating the bumpy roads and plank bridges,

especially in the dark, and he had not travelled that way before.
One bridge was broken and Kimweli found a large log to
repair it and then guided John over it. It was a long and slow
journey, and scary with the noises of the forest at night. The tall
mahogany and redwood trees obscured the moon and stars, and
the headlights of the vehicle did not seem very bright.

They thanked God when they arrived safely at the hospital.
The mother and baby were taken to the maternity unit to be
checked, and the doctor praised Lydia for doing such a good
delivery.

As it was so late, it was decided that everyone should stay
overnight. Lydia and John were invited to the doctor's home,
while Penina and Shairi stayed in the hospital ward with the
mother, who was terrified at the thought of sleeping in a bed—
something she had never seen in her life. They slept under her
bed and the baby was in a little cot nearby. Kimweli slept in the
truck, wanting to guard it for John.

The doctor and his wife were from America, but they had an
English medical student staying with them. He was due to fly
back to the UK the following week. When Lydia heard this, she
thought at once that maybe he could take a letter to Song-Wei
from them.

'I would be delighted to do that,' Jason told them. 'I'm
returning to Southampton to see my parents and be in isolation
before I go back to the hospital in London. I've not had much
contact with them, living out here in the forest, but when I did

go to Kinshasa, I phoned them and heard news that the Covid-19 pandemic has spread all over our country.

Do you need paper and an envelope?'

'Yes please,' Lydia answered, explaining about their daughter in boarding school in Devon.

'I hear that Devon is one of the least affected parts of the country. Covid-19 has been spreading more in the large cities and towns,' he explained, hoping that would reassure the parents, as he went to his room to get the things Lydia needed.

She settled to write a long letter to her daughter, telling her about the Congo, and the news from her grandparents in China, which had arrived recently. She explained all about Grandma and Grampa Lee's work at the hospital, and how Grandpa had become sick, but was slowly getting better. Then she explained that they would now be staying in the Congo for a couple of years, but hopefully she would be able to join them for the long holidays, as they would return to China each year for a long vacation.

'We pray every day for you. Look to Jesus and read from your Bible. He will always be with you. We know that you will be working hard at school.

With all our love,

Mum and Dad.'

Lydia and John were tired after the long day, but they wanted to talk to the American doctor and his wife about their plans to stay on and work in the new hospital which was being built.

'We are Christians,' John explained, 'and we both feel this is what God wants us to do. I used to pastor a small church in our home in China, but life is difficult for Christians in our country, and our small church is not able to continue now that we have moved here. Living here, we hope we could also help the local church, as well as doing our work in the hospital.'

'That is wonderful,' the doctor exclaimed. 'We have been praying for that area of the forest for years and were delighted when we heard a hospital was being built. I will support you in any way I can.

'Once you start admitting patients, we have a short-wave radio schedule at noon each day, so you can contact me if you need advice or have problems. I think this difficult birth you encountered today was in God's plan to bring us together. Let's pray together before we all go to rest.'

Early the next morning, even before it was properly light, everyone gathered to travel back to the village. The doctor, his wife and Jason, the medical student, helped load the truck, giving everyone hot, fresh bread to eat on the way. They prayed for a safe and easy journey, and a blessing on the new baby.

John and Lydia started singing hymns in Mandarin, as they were so full of happiness because of the blessings they had received. Then Penina and Kimweli joined in with songs of their own, trying to teach them to the Chinese couple. The journey was easier in the daylight and they were even back in time for John to collect the other Chinese workmen from the village and get to the hospital for the morning shift.

. When John had his next scheduled broadcast with his supervisor in Kinshasa, he knew the answer he would give. He and Lydia would stay and work in the new hospital.

The 'bush telegraph' had indeed been busy, and Shairi's father was waiting with the night guard in his little shelter by John and Lydia's house.

Shairi and her mother began to tell their story and show him his little son. Penina went to the kitchen, started the fire and boiled water for tea. The little family, Penina, Kimweli and Lydia all sat on the verandah together drinking tea, while the baby was fed. At Oicha hospital, the mother had been given some baby clothes and a blanket, of which she was very proud.

'When our son is named, he should be called Yohanna, named for the Chinese man whose wife has helped me,' she stated. Her husband agreed, and Shairi clapped her hands.

'May we come and visit you?' asked Lydia, and Penina translated for her. 'You will always be welcome, and you can sing your songs to us,' she was told. Lydia felt that confirmed God would use them to help the Pygmies in the Ituri Forest.

– Chapter seventeen –

Somerset

One afternoon the phone rang and Annelise ran to answer it, thinking it might be a call from someone in the village who needed the Helping Hands service.

'Oh, good afternoon, Miss Boston,' Annelise said, when she heard her headmistress speak. 'Are we able to return to school?'

'Sadly, not yet,' she answered, 'but I would like a chat with your mother. Is she available?'

Anneliese ran to get her mother from her office and handed the phone to her.

'I have a couple of things which I need to talk over with you,' she said. 'Firstly, following the death of Song-Wei's guardian and the difficult situation she is in, I want to check that you are still happy about her staying with you. This lockdown appears to be going to last much longer than we thought at first it would. I do not want you to feel you must keep her with you.'

'Don't worry about that,' replied Mrs Lacey. 'She is no trouble at all and a wonderful companion for Annelise. We will keep her until school restarts, however long that might prove to be.'

'That is so kind of you and Dr Lacey and I am sure she will be happy with that arrangement,' replied Miss Boston. 'Now there is another thing. I have a letter from China to forward to her, but also one posted here in the UK. I would like to ask Song-Wei if I can open it before I forward it as well, just in case it is some sort of scam.'

Mrs Lacey went up to the schoolroom where Song-Wei was practising her violin.

Song-Wei was a little apprehensive when she heard that the headmistress wished to talk to her. Was there bad news from home? That was always a niggling fear which had worsened since the pandemic. She was so far away from her family.

'Hello, Miss Boston,' she said politely, taking the phone from Mrs Lacey.

'First of all, I want to tell you that Mrs Lacey would like you to stay with Annelise until school reopens, even if it is a long time. She loves having you as a guest.'

'There is one more thing, Song-Wei,' and Miss Boston explained to her about the letter which had been sent to the school for her.

'Yes, please open it,' responded Song-Wei, who had no idea who might have written to her.

Miss Boston opened the letter and saw there was a letter in English but also one in Chinese script. She read the one in English which was from Jason, who had returned from the Congo with the letter from Song-Wei's mother.

'Someone has brought a letter to England from your parents in the Congo,' she told her pupil. 'I'll send them both to you—I should be able to get to the post office before the last collection and hopefully you will receive it tomorrow—and one has arrived from China, too.'

'Thank you so much. I'm very grateful,' she answered.

Song Wei was so excited she found it hard to sleep that night—to have a letter directly from her Mum was amazing.

Song-Wei's hands were shaking when she opened her letters. The package arrived quite late in the day—the post was somewhat irregular because of the pandemic. She was excited, but also a little scared. She had no idea if the news was good or bad. Part of her wanted to run to her room and read it privately, but another part of her wanted her friends to be with her, so she decided to sit at the kitchen table.

Song-Wei read the Chinese script and every now and then she stopped and told Annelise and her mother a summary of what she was reading. The first letter was from her grandmother.

'Grandma and Grandpa Lee volunteered to help at a hospital which treats patients with Covid-19. Grandma Lee is working in the kitchen as a cook; Grandpa was working as a porter, but then became very sick having caught the virus. He was on a ventilator but is now slowly getting better.'

'And that's like Will,' interrupted Annelise.

'Grandma and Grandpa were given a small room in the nurses' home because it was too far for them to travel each day and they sometimes worked different shifts.

'They had planned to stay and work until the pandemic was over, but now that Grandpa is sick, Grandma thought they should go back to their old apartment. It would be hard for them as they don't have my parents to help them, and they live in an apartment on the third floor, without a lift. When Grandma went to tell the administrator that they could no longer work as volunteers, he was so kind and offered them a bungalow in the hospital grounds, where Grandpa can still have help until he is quite well. Grandma Lee says there is one condition—that she still makes them her chicken dish sometimes, as everyone loves it! That's the recipe which I make for you, the one she taught me,' she added, and they all laughed.

'That must be such a comfort for you to know that they are safe and well and in a better place,' Mrs Lacey said, smiling at Song-Wei. 'I don't expect they hear or see news, so they may not know that the pandemic has spread over here or that your guardian caught Covid-19 in Hong King and died.'

'Yes, they have just heard about Aunt Wong-Jong, and that's why Grandma Lee wrote. She wanted to make sure I knew. It's hard for her to write as she had little education.

'I'm going to keep this letter with my treasures. I don't know when I will see my family again, but I can read this often and think of my grandparents and pray for them.'

Then, with slightly trembling hands, Song-Wei opened the other letter. Her mum's familiar handwriting looked so beautiful with the Chinese characters carefully formed. A lump came to her throat—oh how she longed to be able to hug her mum and dad!

Slowly she read the letter, translating at the end of each paragraph. Her mum told her about living in the forest and how primitive things were. She was honest about her fear of some of the creepy-crawlies and snakes, but also told her about the lovely people in the village and how she was trying to learn the language. She also told her the story of the baby that she delivered, and how that had changed her attitudes.

'We have agreed to stay on here for a year or two,' she wrote, 'but we can go each year to China for holidays. We can do that at the time when you have your long holiday, so that we meet up there, or you could even come here. You might find that challenging, but I think it would also be an exciting experience. We could save up so that we could all have a trip to see the Lowland Mountain Gorillas, which would be amazing.

'The coronavirus has not reached this remote part of Congo, but we hear that it is spreading in England. We pray for your safety and wellbeing every day, and we love you with all our hearts. Stay close to Jesus—that is the most important thing in life.'

As she finished reading the letter, a few tears trickled down her cheeks. The Congo was so far away and they had no internet or phone signals, and she missed her parents so much. Mrs Lacey gave her a big hug.

'That's a hug from your parents,' she said, 'and one day I hope to get the chance to say thank you to them for lending you to our family. I'm so glad you have had this lovely letter from them. Maybe if you write a letter back, the medical student will know a possible way to get it to the Congo without it having to go to China first and be sent with the firm's mail?'

'That would be so cool,' Song-Wei answered. 'Jason gives a telephone number, so I could ring and ask. Do you think that would be ok?'

'I'm sure it would. Why don't you try now while I help Annelise with supper?'

Annelise was the cook that evening and had already prepared most of the meal, so she and her mother finished the cooking while Song-Wei telephoned Jason. She felt very shy about phoning a stranger but did want to talk to him about her parents. Her fears were needless because Jason was kind and helpful. He suggested that she wrote a letter every week to her parents and sent it to him. Then, each month, he would send them to the hospital where he had worked because he knew the post arrived in Kinshasa and once a month was taken to Oicha by a small plane, along with other supplies. From there, it could be sent with a 'runner' through the forest to their village. That was such a good idea and Song-Wei wanted to start as soon as she could. There was so much she wanted to tell her family about life in lockdown at Barrow House.

'Now we have had a long and exciting day, and it's time for bed. Let's just pray for everyone in both of our families now. Tomorrow we can read the book Mr Hodges has lent us and, as the forecast is for hot, dry weather, I wondered if you both would like to have a sleep over in the tree house and do some badger watching?' suggested Mrs Lacey.

'Yay! Can we really?' shouted Annelise, running and giving her Mum a hug. 'That will be so cool!'

'That sounds exciting. I have never seen a badger in real life,' responded Song-Wei.

'I'm not promising that you will see them, but they are usually quite active at the bottom of the garden among the trees. You can see the holes which are entrances to their sets and if you look hard enough, their scratching trees,' Mrs Lacey told her.

It had been a long day and Song-Wei was tired, but she was so very thankful to have heard news of her parents and learn that they were happy and well and, like Will, Grandpa Lee was recovering, when he could so easily have died from the coronavirus.

- CHAPTER EIGHTEEN -

Somerset

The next day was Saturday, so with no schoolwork to do, the girls had more time to research the history of both Barrow House and the treasure they had discovered. Annelise planned to bake a cake for Sunday tea and she decided to try and make bread for the first time. While she was making the cake and setting the bread dough to rise, Song-Wei went to check the greenhouse to see if the tomatoes and cucumbers needed any water and to pick some fresh flowers for the house. Mrs Lacey had been showing her how to arrange them, and she wanted to surprise her by doing a large display for the hallway.

When the girls had finished, they began to read the book that Mr. Hodges had loaned them. Annelise read it aloud to Song-Wei, who did her best to make a few notes so that she would remember the history. It was hard for her since she did not always understand the old-fashioned English words.

'Barrow House has a long history. Originally, there was a Tudor manor house on the site, with timber beams and a small moat around it. This house had been a gift from the King of England to one of his favoured noblemen, Sir Percival Patten and his wife, Lady Madelaine, along with the surrounding land which contained two farms, the small village of Summerfield— where there were about a dozen or so workers' cottages—and a stone church dedicated to St. Mary.

'Sir Percival and Lady Madelaine had two sons, Percy and Sidney. Percy became an officer in the army and Sidney entered the navy. Both sadly died as young adults, Percy from 'congestion on the lungs' and Sidney drowned when his ship was wrecked in a storm. The couple were heartbroken and it is recorded that they became recluses in the manor until their deaths,' read Annelise.

'That's so sad,' said Song-Wei, 'but what does "becoming a recluse" mean?'

Annelise explained to the best of her ability, then took a deep breath and began to read more.

'After their death, the house was occupied by various families and eventually bought by the McDougal family, who had previously lived in Selkirk, Scotland. The house was in need of renovation, and it was Hamish McDougal who renovated the house in 1720. The existing manor house was pulled down, and the moat filled in. A nicely proportioned Georgian House was built on the old foundations. This took some years to complete and at great expense, so, to pay for the renovations, one of the farms was sold and the estate lands considerably reduced.

'The garden was landscaped, including a walled kitchen-garden which supplied the house with vegetables, while the Home Farm produced meat, eggs and milk.'

'So that's when this house was built,' said Annelise. 'I bet it was cold in winter—they had no central heating then, only log fires in the large fireplaces. I guess they must have cooked over a fire in the kitchen. Imagine that! Talking about cooking, I must see how the bread is doing.'

Once she was satisfied that the bread was ready for baking, Annelise returned to read more of the book. She had never been interested in history lessons at school, but since this was about the house where she lived, she found it was a different matter.

'Hamish McDougal and his wife, Flora, left Scotland because, at that time, there was a lot of unrest in the Scottish borders. They bought this house in Somerset wanting to become sheep farmers and be involved in the flourishing wool industry. Flora was not in good health and it was hoped that the milder climate in the West Country might help her to become stronger. Hamish and Flora had two daughters, Elspeth and Iona. Elspeth was like her father, enjoying outdoor activities, especially horse riding, but Iona, like her mother, was not strong, and she died of consumption in her early teens. There is a memorial in the village church to her and her grave can be found in the churchyard.

'A few months later, Flora also died from the same disease. For a while, the house was left uninhabited with all the furniture covered in dust sheets. Hamish took Elspeth to his sheep farm in Combe Down near Bath, where they lived in the farmhouse. Elspeth was fifteen years old and missed her mother and sister very much. She tried to look after her father as best she could.

'After two years, Hamish remarried. His new wife was called Sophia Baker. She was quite young and was more like an older sister than a stepmother to Elspeth, and they became great friends. Elspeth was so fond of her that she decided to add her stepmother's name to her own and became Elspeth McDougal-Baker.

'It was after the marriage of Sophia and Hamish that the family returned to Barrow House.

Elspeth was now a graceful young lady in her late teens. She became part of the Bath social scene, enjoying the promenades and dances.

'One evening, at a ball in the Assembly Rooms in Bath, Elspeth was introduced to a young man called Francis Wicks. It seemed to be love at first sight, and Francis asked her father if he could call at Barrow House and court Elspeth. It was common for girls to marry quite young, and she married Francis in 1731. Following their marriage, the couple moved to Bradford-on-Avon, a wool town in Wiltshire.

'Francis had studied at Oxford University with a view to becoming an ordained minister in the Church of England. After his ordination he was invited to be the curate of a church in a small village just outside Bradford-on-Avon and, although the salary was small, Elspeth's father had provided her with a substantial dowry, and she had inherited her own mother's jewels.'

'Yay!' shouted Song-Wei. 'Those must be the jewels I found!'

'It would seem so,' said Mrs Lacey, who had been in the room and heard some of the story being read. 'I hope we learn more of the family and if any are still traceable.'

A 'ping' disturbed them, and Annelise ran to the kitchen. She opened the oven door, and the wonderful aroma of newly baked bread filled the room. Her bread looked amazing—both her mum and Song-Wei had followed her into the kitchen and gasped in amazement.

'Wow! That's fantastic. I have never made bread in my life,' said her mum. 'I'm so proud of you!'

– CHAPTER NINETEEN –

Somerset

That afternoon Annelise finished icing the sponge cake she had made for the weekend and stood back to admire it. She wished all her dorm mates could have a slice of the bread she made that morning. She took photos of her work and posted it on social media—at least Daisy and Florence could see it! She felt so happy there was something in which she excelled. She was no longer the girl who felt useless at everything.

She put the cake in the middle of the kitchen table alongside the bread, hoping that Song-Wei would soon be back from visiting Mr Hodges, when she heard a car drive through the gates and up to the door. Mum was upstairs in her office, working, so she was surprised when she heard the front door opening.

She ran into the hall and was overjoyed to see her dad.

Annelise instinctively went to give him a hug, but her dad warned her not to do that.

'I'm here for the weekend,' he told her, 'but we still have to be careful. I wanted to surprise you all, so even Mum doesn't know!'

'James, what a lovely surprise,' called her Mum, running down the stairs two at a time to greet her husband.

'No hugs, sweetheart,' he warned her, 'but I felt I couldn't spend another weekend alone at the hospital. Things have eased a little and for the sake of my mental health I have taken the whole weekend off—that is, unless I get paged to go in for a dire emergency. I'll have to sleep in Will's room, but it's so good to come home!'

'Dad, I'm so glad you are here. I didn't know, but I have baked bread for the first time, and made a cake for tea—you can share them,' promised Annelise.

'I thought I could smell something amazing when I came through the door. Mum's been telling me what a great cook you are. I'm so proud of you!' Annelise beamed at his praise.

They all went into the kitchen and Mum put the kettle on.

'Where's Song-Wei?' asked her dad.

'She's visiting Mr Hodges,' answered Annelise. 'He teaches her about plants, and she looks after the greenhouse for him.'

'We have so much to tell you, James,' said his wife. 'The girls have been finding out about the treasure we discovered in the wardrobe when we were spring cleaning. We'll show you this evening.'

'I'm back,' called Song-Wei, as she entered the back door and came into the kitchen.

'Oh, Uncle James! I saw a car in the drive and thought we had a visitor. Good afternoon, Uncle James,' she said politely, not quite sure how she should greet him.

'Hello Song-Wei,' he answered. 'I'm here for the weekend, but we have to be careful about not touching each other and things like that. However, it's so good to be home. After tea, you can show me the greenhouse. I hear Mr Hodges is teaching you about plants. But first, I can't wait to try a slice of that wonderful looking bread, followed by a slice of cake! Can I have the crust, with butter and jam?'

Mrs Lacey laughed. 'You sound just like Will—he always loved the crust!'

After tea and a visit to the greenhouse, the girls got their things together and took them to the treehouse for their sleepover. They made everything ready while it was still light. Not far from the treehouse was a fire pit with some benches around it and that evening it had already been decided to have a barbeque outside—so Annelise's father prepared the fire and her mother the food. It was such a fun evening together and for an hour or two everyone forgot about the Covid-19 virus. They chatted and laughed, telling each other silly jokes, as well as catching up on all the news.

'When we've cleared up from our meal, please show me the treasure you have found,' asked Dr Lacey. 'I can't wait to see it.'

'Wow,' he exclaimed when he was shown the treasure. 'I think these jewels look extremely valuable. As soon as you finish your research into the family of Elspeth, if no-one can be traced as a descendant, then I think they might have to be declared as treasure trove.'

'What does that mean, Uncle?' Song-Wei asked.

'It means that, with treasure, 'finders are not keepers', as some people might hope, but it is divided between the state and the finder.

'Oh, thank you,' responded Song-Wei, not completely sure she understood. She decided to ask Annelise to explain more when they were on their own.

Dr Lacey escorted the girls to the tree house, made sure they were happy and safe and then went to spend the rest of the evening with his wife.

'What a blessing it has been for Annelise to have Song-Wei here,' he commented to his wife. 'I am now certain that this virus isn't going to disappear quickly, and lockdown will continue for the rest of the school year.'

'She has been a blessing to me, too,' Annelise's Mum answered. 'She has made me think about God again and I have been discovering a long-lost faith, as we pray together before bed. How would you feel if we promised to be her English guardians while she is at St. Catherine's? She won't be able to return to China until this pandemic is over. I have talked to Miss Boston about the possibility of a bursary. Song-Wei is a bright student, and it would be such a shame if she had to leave. We can afford to give her pocket money and keep her through the holidays, can't we?'

'I wanted to speak to you about that,' replied Dr Lacey. 'I was going to suggest the same thing to you. It's often been lonely for Annelise since Will and Isobel left home and they do seem to be such good friends.'

'That's settled then. I'll speak to Miss Boston about the possibilities on Monday, after we've talked to Song-Wei to see if she would like that arrangement.'

The girls were excited about their night in the tree house. The woods were quite a distance from the main house, so it felt like a real adventure. They chatted together until it was dark. Then, armed with torches, they climbed down the ladder and sat very quietly on a large log and waited.

After a while they heard a scratching sort of noise and a large badger appeared from a hole a few yards away. He seemed to look around as if wanting to see the coast was clear, then went to a tree trunk and began scratching it, to sharpen his claws. This seemed like a sign because very soon a smaller badger came out of the set, followed by two babies, who started to run around and play. It was enchanting to watch them, and the girls sat very still, not wanting to frighten them away. Then the badger family started to scratch in the ground for grubs and beetles—they made quite a noise munching them.

After a while, the girls heard a rustling sound which came from behind them. They both turned round, and there was a pair of eyes staring at them. Song-Wei almost screamed, but Annelise whispered to her, 'It's only a fox.'

They watched the fox as he darted off further into the woods. It seemed as if the woods became alive at night and it was magical! They heard a screech owl calling out and saw a barn owl swoop down to the ground, catching a small creature.

After watching the animals for over an hour, they began to feel cold and stiff and decided it was time for bed. As they moved to climb the ladder, the animals scattered—no doubt scared by the noise they were making, even though they were trying to keep quiet.

It had been a wonderful experience, and back in the tree house they talked about it for a long time before finally falling asleep. Song-Wei knew she would write about it in the 'lockdown' diary she was keeping and in her letter to her parents. She would never forget the magic of that night.

– CHAPTER TWENTY –

Somerset and Canada

It was a fun weekend spent with Annelise's dad. The family played games together in the swimming pool, a sort of 'water volleyball' with the girls playing against the adults. The weather stayed fine, and they were able to have a second barbeque in the woods, and the girls showed the adults where they had seen the badgers playing.

In the evening, Annelise read some more of the book Mr Hodges had lent them. They wrote down the important details, and then recounted to Dr Lacey all they had found out.

Annelise continued to read aloud from the account which Mr Hodges' great grandfather had written.

'After two years of marriage, Elspeth returned to Barrow House to stay with her father and stepmother while her husband, Francis, took a trip to Canada. He felt his life's work was to look after a small congregation of settlers and trappers in the north of the country. The plan was that Elspeth would join him once he had built a log cabin and established a church. As her stepmother was expecting a baby, she was glad to return home to help.

'It took months for letters from Francis to reach her, so she had to wait patiently. Elspeth was delighted when her half-sister was born. The little girl was named Sarah Anne and Elspeth became her godmother. Very sadly, during the first winter after her birth, she became ill with pneumonia and died. She, too, is buried in the graveyard of the village church.'

'That's so sad,' said Song-Wei.' It must have been terrible for all the family.'

'At that time in history, many children died because much less was understood about the human body and illness, and it wasn't until 1940's that antibiotics were widely accessible,' Dr Lacey explained to her.

'What happened next?' asked Mrs Lacey.

Annelise read on.

'The next record we have is that Elspeth sailed to Canada in May 1735 to join her husband, only to discover that he had died from a fever just a month before she arrived. She knew that she would not be able to survive alone in the wilds of Northern Canada, so she packed up his few possessions, with the help of a friend of her late husband, and as soon as she could she travelled back to England.

'Once again, she returned to Barrow House to live and remained there for the rest of her life. Elspeth outlived her father and stepmother. While she had been in Canada, a half-brother, Arthur McDougal, had been born. He grew up at Barrow House, and on the death of their parents, the house was bequeathed to him on the condition that Elspeth could live there for as long as she wanted.

'It appears that it was a happy arrangement and, after Elspeth's death in 1781, Arthur and his wife, Margaret, continued to live in Barrow House and farm the sheep in Combe Down.

'Members of the McDougal family continued to live at Barrow House until the outbreak of World War I. At that time, it belonged to Mrs Lucy McDougal Grey and her husband, Gerald. Gerald was an army officer in the Somerset Light Infantry, and the upkeep of the house became too much for Lucy since most of the household staff had joined the war effort to help in one way or another. So, she allowed the house to become a convalescent home for wounded soldiers and moved to live in a cottage in the village.

'Gerald was killed at the Battle of the Somme and Lucy was broken-hearted. She did not want to return to live on her own in Barrow House. So, after the war, Lucy sold the house and emigrated to a small town called Manitou, in Manitoba, Canada.'

'Isn't that strange,' interrupted her mum. 'I wonder if she knew of her family connection with Canada all those years before?'

'This is the end of Revd. Hodges little booklet, but there are some notes added in handwriting.

'The next owners of Barrow House were Frank and Ada Noble, and they did major renovations both to the house and garden,' Annelise continued to read out loud. 'They had five children: Ivy, Gwendoline, Mabel, Winifred and Frederick. After Frank and Ada died, Frederick inherited the property in 1956. He was a veteran of the Second World War and had sustained horrific physical and mental trauma in Japan as a prisoner of war. My father, Ernest Hodges, became his gardener and helped with maintenance jobs around the house. They became good friends since they were both war veterans. I joined the garden team in 1968 when I was 16 years old, and worked there continuously until 2020 aged 70 years, when a virus called Covid-19 hit the British Isles and made me become a prisoner in my own home. The present owners, Dr and Mrs Lacey, moved here in 1999 and have brought Barrow House into the twenty-first century.'

Annelise took a deep breath, and then added, 'That bit is signed by Bill Hodges.'

'That's given us a good history of the house, and we know what happened to Elspeth and Francis,' commented Mrs Lacey. 'We will need to research Lucy McDougal Grey who went to Canada in 1919. If she remarried, then she may have had children who would be her descendants, and the treasure would be theirs, I guess.'

'It would be good to photocopy this history before we return it to Mr Hodges,' decided Dr Lacey. 'It's part of our history now.'

'What about the letters?' asked Song-Wei. 'Will we still read those?'

'I think it will be interesting to do so, and then we'll keep them in case we trace Lucy's ancestors—I'm sure they would want them. Grandma hasn't yet sent me any gloves. I still think we need to use gloves when we handle them as they are so old,' commented Mrs Lacey.

'Phone Grandma tonight,' suggested Dr Lacey. 'If she can't find any old cotton gloves, you can buy some latex ones from the chemist in the village and they would be almost as good.'

The girls were very sleepy after the previous night in the tree house followed by the excitement of the day and decided to go to bed early.

'Just before you go up, I'd like to have a chat with Song-Wei,' said Dr Lacey. 'I have to go back to the hospital tomorrow and may not see you all for a few weeks.'

Song-Wei felt a bit nervous. Was Uncle James going to tell her she had stayed with them too long? Had she done something wrong? Maybe he had bad news about her family? She was always afraid of that. Mrs Lacey went upstairs with Annelise, leaving them both in the snug.

'Don't look so worried, Song-Wei. I just want to ask you a question,' Dr Lacey said, with a smile on his face.

'I know that you had sad news about your guardian a few weeks ago. I was wondering how you would feel if Aunt Julia and I became your guardians for the rest of your time at St. Catherine's? It's not easy to contact your parents to ask permission, but I am sure that Miss Boston would agree to the arrangement, because she knows us well as she was Head Mistress when Isobel was there. While you remain in England, our home will always be a home to you, for as long as you need one,' he explained.

Song-Wei gasped in surprise and a huge smile spread over her face.

'Are you sure?' she asked. 'I would so love to stay with you through the holidays, but ...' and then she sighed deeply, '... there is a problem. I have no money to pay for my food or clothes or anything.'

'That is why I wanted to talk to you on your own. Aunt Julia has explained your circumstances and we both want you to know that we will take care of you in every way, just as if you were our daughter. Indeed, we think of you as our foster-daughter already. We hope you can confide in us as you would your parents if you have any worries or needs. We both have good jobs and, even in this present situation with the Covid-19 crisis, we get good salaries and there is plenty of money for us to take care of you. We both love you and are so happy that Annelise has a friend of her own age. It has been lonely for her sometimes, and you are such good friends.'

'We are and have such fun together. I don't know how to say thank you enough. You are both so kind. One day, I hope my parents can meet you to say thank you, too. I have been frightened about what might happen to me. Aunt Julia says that Miss Boston might find money to pay my school fees for St. Catherine's. I promise I'll be good and work hard.'

– CHAPTER TWENTY-ONE –

Somerset

As June progressed, the British government began to ease some of the restrictions, but schools were still not able to reopen. However, people were allowed out and about a little more and shops other than pharmacies and food stores reopened. One day Mrs Lacey decided to take the girls into Bath to show Song-Wei some of the beautiful buildings in the city. One of their set books for English Literature was Pride and Prejudice by Jane Austin, set in the Georgian period in Bath. It made the story seem far more real when they walked around the elegant Georgian buildings. It made them think of Elspeth, too, when she was a teenager and went to dances in the Assembly Rooms in Bath.

They all had to be careful to keep two metres away from other people, regularly sanitizing their hands and much of the time wearing masks, but none of them minded. It was so good to leave the village and see other places. Mrs Lacey promised that, as soon as the Roman Baths and other historical places reopened for visitors, she would take Song-Wei to see them.

By the middle of June, Will was well enough to travel home to convalesce. He was not yet fit enough to drive himself all the way to Higher Summerfield, but a colleague was travelling to Bristol and kindly made a short detour to bring him to Barrow House. The disease had left him weak and so, at times, he needed to use a wheelchair. Because of this, a downstairs room was prepared as a bedroom for him.

Song-Wei cut the nicest flowers that she could find to brighten up the room and as it was Chinese night, she prepared Grandma Lee's chicken dish, while Annelise baked a chocolate cake for tea and a pavlova for dessert. The family were excited that Will was coming home again and determined to help his recovery.

It was great to have some good news at last. Isobel made a video phone call in the evening, introducing Tanner to Will, and showing everyone a beautiful engagement ring! Song-Wei thought to herself that it would have been perfect if only Uncle James had been home, too. She was beginning to feel that Will and Isobel were part of her family, just as Annelise was like a sister to her.

The girls still had to keep to their school timetable, but once lessons were finished for the day, they enjoyed pushing Will into the garden and talking about the treasure they found, and the story they had discovered behind it. Will decided that he would help the girls with the research to discover if Lucy McDougal Grey had ever remarried after she settled in Canada, and if there were any living descendants. It gave him something interesting to do and it was a blessing for the girls as Annelise was spending so much time in the kitchen and Song-Wei in the garden.

By the end of June, Will was able to walk around the garden and take short walks with Goldie. The sunshine and fresh air and all the good food were speeding his recovery.

Miss Boston phoned Mrs Lacey one morning. She apologized that school would now remain closed at least until the Autumn term, but said she was delighted with the work the girls were doing and explained that Annelise would be promoted to the top set for maths, science and English when they returned, and Song-Wei had done so well in English that she now could be in the top set. Then she gave even better news: Song-Wei could return to school because a full bursary had been granted, which would pay for her tuition, boarding fees, and uniform!

'I'm so delighted. Thank you for considering her,' Mrs Lacey replied. 'We know that we cannot be legal guardians because we are not able to get the parental consent, although we are sending a letter to them via the medical student who has a contact, but my husband and I have promised Song-Wei that we will give her a home for however long she needs one in this country. We will provide her pocket money needs. She and Annelise are just like sisters and it's a joy to have her with us.'

'Thank you,' said Miss Boston. 'We do so want to keep her at St. Catherine's. She is already a credit to the school.'

'Guess what?' Mrs Lacey asked Song-Wei, as the girls came down to get lunch ready.

'What is it?' she replied. 'I can see you are happy about something. Have you had good news?'

'Yes, I have very good news for you,' said Mrs Lacey, smiling from ear to ear. 'You have been given a full scholarship at St. Catherine's—tuition, boarding, uniform all paid for!'

'Yay! That's so cool! I won't have to leave at the end of this school year! Thank you so much. I know you asked Miss Boston about such a possibility, but I didn't dare dream it might happen!'

Annelise was also jumping up and down, thrilled for her best friend.

'That's not all the good news,' Mrs Lacey said, and went on to tell them about the good results from all their hard work and the promotion to top sets in most subjects. 'I am so proud of you both and how well you are doing. We'll phone Dad tonight and you can tell him the good news.'

'What good news?' asked Will, coming into the kitchen. 'What's all the excitement about?'

He was so pleased for the girls when he heard about Miss Boston's phone call. 'Never say again that you aren't any good at anything,' he told his young sister. 'Each one of us has some talents, because every person is special.'

Mrs Lacey decided that all this good news deserved a celebration. She planned a garden party and, although it was only possible to invite a few friends, she told the girls they could invite one person each. Song-Wei invited Mr Hodges and Annelise, Maggie from the village shop. They planned to hold it on the following Saturday afternoon because the shop shut at noon. Both girls were looking forward to the party because through lockdown there were so few events happening.

The girls were sent out on their bikes for a long cycle ride that Saturday morning, while Mrs Lacey and Will, with help from a few of the other 'Helping Hands' from the village, set up a gazebo in the garden. The cakes and sandwiches had been ordered from a caterer and everywhere was decorated with bunting and balloons.

Chairs were borrowed from the village hall because they were plastic and easy to sanitize after use. They were placed in such a way that the 'two metre' social distance rule could be observed.

Will had invited his dad who arranged to take time off to come to the party, and Mrs Lacey had invited a 'mystery' guest but was not sure if she would be able to attend.

It was a warm, sunny afternoon, perfect for a garden party, and Song-Wei and Annelise waited by the front gate to escort their guests into the back garden. Mr Hodges was longing to potter in the greenhouse and see all his plants! He was thrilled to see how well 'his' garden was doing! He praised his young apprentice, and she was so happy.

Maggie and Annelise walked into the wood, where Annelise showed her the badger sets and the scratching trees. Will walked to meet his father, when he heard the car come through the drive. They had a few 'father and son' moments together before they joined the others.

Mrs Lacey was just about to pour out the tea for everyone when they heard another car arrive. Her mystery guest had managed to come! She ran to help a spritely elderly lady out of her car and lead her to the garden. It was Grandma! Annelise got up ready to run and hug her but was gently reminded that she could not do that until the pandemic restrictions were lifted.

It was such a happy afternoon. Mrs Lacey explained to the guests what the celebration was all about.

'I just wanted to say a big 'thank you' to Annelise and Song-Wei for all their help through this lockdown,' she said. 'I was dreading the thought of working from home, helping Annelise with schoolwork and coping with cooking, housework and the garden all by myself. Then Annelise asked if her school friend, Song-Wei, could come and stay, as she was unable to go home to China. The two of them have been wonderful. They have helped with the cooking and gardening, and we have discovered our daughter is a wonderful cook, and our 'foster' daughter a wonderful gardener.

The girls had the bright idea of setting up 'Helping Hands' in the community. This has been a huge success and spread from our village to many others around here. James and I are so proud of both girls, and we want to thank Mr Hodges and Maggie for their help—both in their own way have helped the girls develop their talents. We have coped with the Covid-19 crisis and Will is back with us well on his way to resuming full health. Isobel stayed in The Gambia to help with the pandemic and has met the love of her life and recently become engaged to a young man called Tanner, so we have much to celebrate. Enjoy your tea!'

Everyone clapped, and then feasted on all the lovely food which had been prepared for them.

Grandma had turned out her bedroom drawers and found the cotton gloves which were needed by the girls to handle the old letters, much to their delight. It was the first outing Grandma had been able to make since the beginning of lockdown, and the family were so delighted to see her in real life and not just on the computer screen! They were all missing hugs, though, and longing for the social distancing to end for good.

Everyone's spirits were lifted by the garden party and they felt happy and more hopeful that the country was now recovering and life was becoming normal once again.

– CHAPTER TWENTY-TWO –

Somerset

One afternoon, at the end of June, the Vicar came to visit. Now that small social gatherings were permitted, he could visit his parishioners to see them face to face, although still socially distanced.

The girls and Will were swimming in the pool when he arrived, so Mrs Lacey took him into the garden, and they sat and talked for a while watching the young people having fun together.

'I heard that your family had grown,' commented the Vicar. 'Mr Hodges told me about his young friend and how she has looked after his precious plants.'

'Yes, Song-Wei had nowhere to go when lockdown began, so we invited her here. She is a delight—a great companion for Annelise—and both girls have been helping in lots of ways. Her father was a pastor in China, but his little church had to close when his work took him abroad. He works as a structural engineer for a construction company and he and his wife were sent to head up a project in the Democratic Republic of Congo, to build a hospital. The project is almost completed, but they have been asked to stay on, her father to be the administrator and her mother to help set up the nursing services there. They have agreed to do this for a couple of years. Her grandparents are still in China and her grandfather has been very sick with Covid-19, but he is slowly recovering now.'

'It has been a troubling and disturbing time for us, hasn't it?' the Vicar commented. 'Many of my parishioners have been perplexed, but it has made them think about the big issues of life and death. We have been having an online service and I have been pleased because a lot of people have tuned in who would not normally come to church. This time is making people think of the big issues of life and death and what is really important.'

"I found an online service from the Chinese church in London and Song-Wei has loved taking part each week. She has taught me to pray again—something I had not done much since my childhood. We pray together before bed and, when Will was so sick, it was such a comfort. I know now that God is real and has answered our prayers. When all this is over and you are holding services again, we will come along. Mr Hodges told us that you were holding a course to help people understand the Christian faith. If you do that again, I will try to come and so will James. I know Song-Wei wants to be baptized—I think she has already chosen a Christian name for herself ready for that event,' said Mrs Lacey, with a smile.

Once the young people had showered and dressed, they all had tea together in the garden. As the Vicar took a bite into the scones which Annelise had made earlier, he told her that her fame as a cook was growing throughout the village. She blushed with pride. It was so cool to have found something in which she could excel and that had helped her confidence grow.

'I want to thank you girls,' he said, 'for your great idea of the "Helping Hands" scheme. I know you have been a blessing to the community. You have reminded us grown-ups of how we need to care for each other, and I am praying that the scheme will continue, even after the crisis is over. Many people are isolated and lonely, especially in a rural community like ours, and I have lots of ideas of how the church family can get involved and help, once the restrictions are fully lifted. Some of our elderly folk were already imprisoned by loneliness long before the Covid-19 crisis came along.'

After tea, the girls escorted the Vicar to the front gate.

'Thank you for calling,' Song-Wei said. 'When we are all "unlocked" again, may I talk to you about being baptized? My parents wanted me to be sure of my faith before I took this step. One reason for my coming to England for school was so that I would not be brainwashed in the Chinese state schools but make up my own mind about faith. While I have been here, I have read my Bible each day and found Jesus to be real to me in a new way. When my guardian died and before I heard that my family are still alive in China and the Congo, I felt so alone, just like an orphan. Now I know for sure I am in the family of God and He will take care of me. I am part of this lovely family here, too, and am so grateful. I know that is a gift from God to me and a promise that He will always look after me.'

Annelise stared at her friend, tears in her eyes. She had never known her friend to say such a long speech!

'Yay! You're my foster sister now,' she said. 'We all love you so much. You have been teaching us to love God, too.'

'Your mother told me that,' said the Vicar, 'and I was so pleased to hear that you pray together. As soon as it is possible, in keeping with the government guidelines, we will arrange a baptismal class for you. God bless you and thanks for the delicious tea and a lovely afternoon. Keep praying that this virus will soon be defeated, and life will get back to normal again, where we do not need to mask our faces or keep our distance from each other.'

- CHAPTER TWENTY-THREE -

Canada

Will was as good as his word and researched Lucy's journey to Manitou. He contacted the record offices in that town and found that three years after her arrival she was granted Canadian citizenship.

Then Will found Lucy was mentioned in the local newspaper when she became engaged to be married to a Mr Thomas Holm. From there he was directed to the records of the Episcopal Church in Manitou and discovered that, on 1 October 1923, her wedding to Thomas was recorded.

The next entries relating to the family were baptisms—1925, Barbara Lucy Holm was baptized; 1927, Thomas (Junior) Samuel Holm was baptized; and 1931, Susan Anne-Marie Holm's baptism was recorded.

After that, it became a little more complicated to trace the family, but the records officer was extremely helpful and promised to continue to research them.

At tea-time every afternoon, Will updated his mum and the girls with the information he had gleaned, and he drew up a family tree.

Barbara became a schoolteacher, and in 1945 she married and moved to Winnipeg. There were no records of any children.

Thomas Junior joined the Royal Mounted Police and had a very successful career. Sadly, he died in a car accident in 1967, a few months before he was due to be married.

One afternoon Will had more exciting news.

'We're really getting close now,' he told them. 'Susan, Lucy's youngest daughter married in 1953. Her husband, Alan Paulson, was a prairie wheat farmer. He died in 1993 and Susan in 2011. They had a daughter called Jayne, but the researcher hasn't yet been able to discover what happened to her. They also produced twin sons, Derek and David, born in 1958, who eventually took over the farm.

They would be over 60 now, so maybe have retired or sold the farm, but if I can track down the twins, we will have found descendants of Elspeth.'

Having heard this news, and now that some of the lockdown restrictions had been lifted, allowing people to travel further afield, Mrs Lacey decided that she would make an appointment with one of her school friends who now worked in the Victoria and Albert Museum in London and show her the jewellery they had found, to get some sort of idea as to the value and what they ought to do next.

Meanwhile, with gloved hands, the girls were reading Elspeth's letters from her husband, Francis after he had sailed to Canada.

He told her how sad he felt, even though he was excited, as he embarked for Canada.

'I couldn't bear the sight of seeing you standing at the quay at Southampton. You looked so sweet in your blue dress and waving your lace handkerchief. I wanted to run down the gang plank and take you in my arms and go home with you. It was upsetting to see you becoming smaller and smaller in the distance. Had I not known that God had called me to work in the New World, I could not have borne the loss of leaving you behind. My only solace now is that as soon as I can, I will build us a cabin and you can join me. Then it will be an adventure for us both,' read Mrs Lacey—and all of them felt tears in their eyes as she did so.

The next letter told his wife about the sea journey.

'For many days, while in the Bay of Biscay, I lay in my cabin, unable to eat or drink. The motion of the sea made me so nauseated. I felt so miserable, as did the other three men who share this cabin. Now the weather has cleared, and the sea is calm. Make sure you bring some smelling salts and ginger biscuits. I suggest you see if the doctor can prescribe you something to help seasickness, should it occur when you travel to join me.

'The three men with me are all bachelors still. They hope to find wealth in Canada, make a fortune and find good wives. They laugh at me in derision when they hear that I am a minister of the Gospel and my aim is to tell people about Jesus and His love for them, whatever their race or colour of skin. However, they are not vicious, and we get along quite nicely.'

'That is like my father when he was pastor of the little church in China,' commented Song-Wei. 'Many people laughed at him, some even spat at him and called him names, because he wanted to tell people about Jesus. They could not understand why he would send me, his only child, to a foreign country to be educated and have the choice to make up my own mind about religion.'

'He is very brave, Song-Wei, and we respect all we hear about him,' Annelise told her.

'I have arrived! the next letter stated. 'Oh, how good it is to stand on 'terra firma' again! I am thankful to be in the country of my calling, even though I miss you more each passing day. I pray that we will soon be reunited, my dearest.

'Now begins the long trek north. Much of it will be difficult terrain. I bade farewell to my fellow passengers, who are going west to farm in the prairies.

'I needed to buy supplies for my journey and tools to make a home for you. They are in a covered wagon and I hope to be part of a wagon train which will leave in a day or so. We must be on our way as soon as we can because, in Canada, the summers are short and hot, but the winters are long and very cold. I have a coat made of seal skin—it should keep me warm when winter comes. I can see already that this is a beautiful land. God has blessed it indeed. You will love it, I am sure.

'This may be the last letter for a few months as there are few mail depots in the north—but when people travel south, they kindly take letters with them. There is a spirit of kindness to strangers and a sense of being brothers as we endure the hardship of conquering this country, going along a path we have never travelled before. Keep in good spirits, dearest. One day I will retrace my steps to meet you off the boat and bring you home. God haste that day. Meanwhile, I love you with all my heart, Francis.'

It seemed sad reading the letters, knowing that Francis was never able to meet her from the boat. Even so, they felt compelled to read the next one.

'We travelled for four months to reach our destination. Now it is winter and devastatingly cold. You must make yourself thick winter underwear, for it is so cold here. Please knit me some thick woollen stockings and bring them with you. You can start to collect things and pack the trunk bit by bit, even as I am building a log cabin little by little. It will not be anything like the houses in England, and very different from Barrow House, but I will make it as cosy as I am able and it will be our love nest where I hope we can raise a family. It will be best not to bring your valuables with you. Find somewhere safe to keep them until our return. This is a wild country, and I would not want you to lose them.

'I work at building the house one or two hours a day. Then I spend the time with the people, getting to know them. I have started a Bible Class for the men and a simple service on Sundays for the families. There is no church building yet, but we meet in various homes and then eat lunch together afterwards. It will be so wonderful to have you by my side once again. 'The women will love you and I am sure they will want a class, and the children a Sunday School.

'All my love dearest Elspeth. Maybe in my next letter I will be able to tell you to buy the ticket for your passage. Your loving husband, Francis.'

The last letter was written eight months later. The writing was less distinct and more difficult for Mrs Lacey to read.

'My beloved Elspeth. I cannot express to you how much I miss you! We approach yet another winter and I cannot bear to think of the long dark days without you. Every day, I look at the painted miniature I have of you and pray for you, and I read your letters over and over. I believe that God is keeping you strong and well. The cabin is ready now and I have a good fireplace which draws well. There is an abundance of wood available, so I have a barn with many logs stored to see me through the winter. I have a cow, too, who should calve in the spring. We will have plenty of milk in the summer. I planted a garden last spring and grew vegetables and fruit, some of which one of our parishioners has preserved for me to use this winter.

'I ask you to buy a ticket for the ship which leaves Southampton in May. That way as soon as the snow melts, I will make the trek in the covered wagon to meet you when the ship docks. We will buy stores in the town and travel home before winter. What celebrations we will have!

'Pray for me, dearest, for I have developed a cough which keeps me awake at night.

'The work is progressing, and several people have asked Jesus into their lives and request baptism. Praise God for His blessing. I constantly pray for you and our families. If it is convenient when this letter finally reaches you, could you ride over to my parents and greet them from me.

'Please God, we will be reunited next year.

All my love dearest wife,

Francis.'

'That is the last letter. I wonder if she managed to get any replies to Francis?' said Mrs Lacey. 'I guess the ships which sailed, took mail and delivered them to the town post office. It might have been months before they reached Francis, but how exciting it would have been to get an answer! It makes me so thankful for modern technology which we can use to email and video call our friends and relatives. The Gambia doesn't seem too far away because we can see and talk to Isobel, and flights only take about five or six hours to reach there.'

'Do you think the safe place she hid the letters and jewellery was where we found them?' asked Song-Wei. 'That wardrobe could have been sold, or chopped up as firewood years ago, and then no one would have known the story.'

'I don't know if they had banks and safe deposit boxes as we know them now,' Will answered. 'Perhaps that seemed the safest place to Elspeth. It's amazing that the wardrobe has stayed in the house for hundreds of years.'

'I always thought it was ugly—quite a monstrosity—but now I think differently,' commented Annelise. 'We must keep it in the house forever and, if we ever move away, I shall write a letter and hide it there for someone else to find.'

'That's really a cool idea, sis,' said Will. 'Maybe we should all write letters now and make it like a time capsule, telling people about the pandemic and being in lockdown for months on end— the year of the mask, as Annelise calls it. I shall write about the illness and what it felt like, thinking I might be dying.'

'Thank God you didn't,' said Annelise. 'And thanks, Song-Wei, for teaching us to pray and have faith in God.'

– Chapter twenty-four –

Herefordshire

The school term ended in the middle of July, and St. Catherine's planned to reopen in the second week of September. People now were feeling more optimistic as restrictions eased and families were able to move around and even go on holiday, so long as the social distancing, wearing of masks in shops and handwashing was observed. Dr Lacey was able to take some leave from work, so the family planned to go to Herefordshire, camping in the Forest of Dean for a week.

'I can't wait,' said Song-Wei. 'I have never been away on a holiday before. The nearest thing was the sleepover in the tree house, and that was so much fun!'

She was not aware that in the second garage there was a camper van, until Will drove it out and started to give it a service. Soon he had everyone helping to clean the inside and learn how to put the roof up and the bunk beds down.

As well as the van, they decided to take two tents—one where the guys would sleep and the other as a sort of living room, should the weather be unkind to them. The tents had to be put up in the back garden to make sure they were in working order and even doing that was an adventure.

'You won't think it fun if we have a howling gale or torrential rain,' laughed Will, as he showed the girls what to do and they were giggling as they struggled to get the tent pegs properly secured.

The family set off on a sunny morning in high spirits. For much of the journey, the Lacey family taught Song-Wei English folk songs, which they sang lustily as they travelled. It was not a particularly long journey, but they still stopped for a picnic on the way, and Goldie had a run.

It was the middle of the afternoon when they arrived and set up the tents on their allotted pitch. There was a fire pit for them to use if they wanted to cook outside, they could hook up to electricity and there was a standing pipe with drinking water. To one side of the site was a shower and toilet block, and on the other side a farm shop which sold fresh milk, bread & other food items. It was quite a small site with about a dozen camping pitches, most of them filled.

Having set up camp, the girls went off to explore while Mrs Lacey visited the farm shop. Will was cook for the evening—Annelise wondered what they would eat as Will was not very domesticated!

Annelise and Song-Wei took Goldie as they set off to explore the part of the forest closest to them. It was warm and sunny, and they enjoyed walking through the trees. Goldie kept exploring, sniffing almost every tree and hole he saw. Suddenly they came across a little stream, so they took off their trainers, rolled up their jeans and paddled. It was delightfully cold, and Goldie soon joined them as they splashed around. He tried to catch some tiny fish which were swimming around—the girls laughed so much because he had no idea what to do except to chase them.

When they got back to the camp there was a great smell of sausages, which Will was cooking over the fire pit. They feasted on sausages and baked beans, and then Will showed them how to make 'smores', which he told them was an American camping speciality. The girls toasted marshmallows and ate them in a sandwich using digestive biscuits. Maybe not the best nutrition—but delicious! Everyone helped clear up and then they sat around the campfire playing a story game.

It was Annelise's idea—something they did in the dorm at school. She started a story by giving a sentence, then the person next to her had to continue it, and so it passed around them all until they ran out of ideas.

At the end of the evening, Mrs Lacey took the girls to the showers while the men put out the fire, before they all found their sleeping bags and settled for the night. Goldie decided he would sleep in the 'sitting room' tent and guard it!

The holiday proved to be hugely successful. The weather was mostly sunny and each day they explored the forest. The pandemic restrictions stopped them going to some places like the Forest Centre, but they found plenty to do. The stream became a favourite place to go, to paddle or swim. Towards the end of the week Will and his dad decided one afternoon to try to tickle some trout to cook over the campfire. Annelise and her Mum went for a walk together, leaving Song-Wei and Goldie in the 'sitting room' because she was complaining of a headache.

She had dozed off to sleep, Goldie at her feet, when suddenly she was woken by a noise outside. Goldie barked, and they both went to see what was happening.

Outside were a couple of youths who were snooping around the camper van.

Song-Wei was glad that she had locked it and had the key in the pocket of her shorts. Goldie growled and Song-Wei challenged the boys. 'What are you doing? Is there something you need?'

She felt a bit scared because she did not much like the look of the guys. She prayed in her head asking the Lord to help her.

'Oh, look who it is,' one said to the other with a sneer. 'A Chinese kid! It's her lot we have to blame for all the trouble with this virus. I bet she brought it over here! Let's teach her a lesson she'll never forget. We don't want foreigners in our country bringing their horrible bugs with them.'

Song-Wei felt her mouth go dry and her limbs shake. She was scared. They looked to be in their late teens and one of them flicked a knife. For a few seconds she felt rooted to the spot—then she decided to run, Goldie at her heels.

She ran into the forest hoping to reach the stream, but the boys were far too big and strong and soon caught her up. She looked round for Goldie, but he had disappeared into the forest.

'Got you!' one boy shouted, grabbing her arm. The other knocked her to the ground. She twisted her ankle as she fell, and pain shot through her.

'Let's have a bit of fun with her before we punish her,' said the boy who held the knife.

Song-Wei was now terrified as he held it near her neck. She tried to pray out loud in Mandarin.

'Lord, help me. You promised you would never leave me,' she whispered.

'Hold your tongue, you stupid foreign kid,' he shouted at her. 'The more noise you make the worse it will be for you!'

The other boy began to dance around her chanting, 'If you go down to the woods today be sure of a great surprise, only it won't be a teddy bears' picnic for you. We'll have more fun than that. By now the boy with the knife was sitting on her, still holding the knife to her neck.

Song-Wei was sure that she might be killed and began to cry.

'Cry baby bunting, daddy's gone a hunting,' chanted the other boy. 'Gone to get a rabbit's skin to wrap his baby bunting in!' as he danced around her with an evil look in his eye.

Both boys laughed at what they thought was a great joke, and then they sang the nursery rhyme time and time again, getting faster and faster. They seemed to be out of control and in a frenzy, so much so that they did not notice or hear Will and Dr Lacey running and Goldie leading them to Song-Wei.

Will grabbed the boy who was dancing round her, and at the same time, Dr Lacey got hold of the other boy, knocking the knife from his hand. They struggled but the men overpowered them. Goldie went to Song-Wei and licked her, but, as she tried to stand up, the pain from her ankle caused her to scream.

146

'Stay still Song-Wei,' said Dr Lacey. 'We'll deal with these boys and Goldie will guard you. Auntie and Annelise are on their way—I phoned as we ran here after Goldie alerted us. Take deep breaths and don't move. Have you got your phone with you?'

Song-Wei nodded and moved slightly to reach into the pocket of her jeans.

'Phone 999 for police and I'll shout as loud as I can to speak to them, but otherwise I'll tell you what to say.'

In fact, Annelise and her mum arrived as she was trying to phone, but her hands were shaking so much that she was glad to hand it to Mrs Lacey who took over the call. It was a good thing that Dr Lacey and Will had both been good at rugby and knew how to tackle and keep the young men in hold.

Annelise sat with Song-Wei, holding her friend's hand, talking gently to her, for the trauma was making her shake all over. She whispered that she was scared that the men would get tired and the boys would escape.

'Jesus will protect you,' said Annelise. 'Mum and I prayed as we ran here when we knew there was a problem, for Goldie would never have left you alone. He knew something was wrong.'

'You're a very clever dog,' she added, giving Goldie a cuddle.

It was such a relief when they heard the police sirens, and Mrs Lacey ran up to the caravan site to meet them and show them where to come and explain briefly what she knew of the situation.

Within minutes the boys were handcuffed and put into police cars. Two detectives then arrived to ask questions, and Dr Lacey explained what he and Will had found when they arrived at the scene. He pointed to the knife which he had knocked out of the boy's hand. The detective carefully put it into a bag for forensics to examine.

Meanwhile a policewoman had come straight to Song-Wei to help her. She tried to stand up, but the pain was unbearable. Her face blanched and she almost fainted.

'I need to call an ambulance for Song-Wei,' she explained to Mrs Lacey. 'Her ankle may be broken. Can you get a blanket from your camp and put around her shoulders? She is shivering and in a state of shock.'

'I will,' said Annelise at once, glad to do something practical to help.

– Chapter twenty-five –

Herefordshire and Somerset

None of the family will ever forget that evening. Will stayed with Song-Wei in the ambulance, and Mrs Lacey followed with the policewoman in a police car. Dr Lacey gave a full statement to the detectives, then looked after Annelise.

Once at the hospital, Song-Wei was tested for Covid-19 before being taken for x-rays. Her ankle was broken, but fortunately it was not a bad fracture requiring pins and plates. Will tried to keep her entertained and told her how it would be plastered.

'I'll be the first to autograph it,' he promised.

Mrs Lacey had to go into great explanations about Song-Wei's relationship to the family and why she was living with them.

The worst ordeal was for Song-Wei to repeat the story of what happened and what the boys had said to her several times. She shook as she recalled the words.

'Thank goodness Dad and I arrived when we did—Goldie could smell the evil intentions of those boys, I'm sure,' Will said. 'God was looking after you.'

The doctors decided that Song-Wei should stay overnight in the hospital and be seen the next morning in the fracture clinic before she could be discharged. Mrs Lacey asked if she could stay with her, and Will returned to the camp.

Once the police had all the information they needed, Dr Lacey thought that everyone should return to Barrow House as soon as possible. The holiday was almost over, and it seemed the most sensible thing to do. The hospital in Bath could take over the care that Song-Wei needed. She had been warned that her ankle would take about six weeks to heal, after which she would need to do exercises to regain full movement. It was sad that the holiday had ended in such a horrible way, but everyone was glad to leave the camp site.

'I'm so sorry,' Song-Wei kept telling everyone. 'If I had gone for a walk with Aunt Julia and Annelise, it wouldn't have happened.'

'It's not your fault,' she was told by everyone. 'No one had any idea that those thugs would try to steal from our camp site, let alone attack you. We all thought you were safe staying there, especially with Goldie to keep you company,' added Mrs Lacey. 'I hope they get put away for a long time,' she added. 'I just keep thanking God that nothing worse happened to you. Your ankle will soon mend.'

'Mum,' said Annelise. 'Can I stay home until Song-Wei goes back to school? We can work from home and I can keep her company.'

'I don't know,' Mrs Lacey answered. 'We can talk it over with Miss Boston. It will mean you lose half of the winter term. It depends if you can still get lessons through the computer.'

Once they were back at Barrow House, they were all quarantined, since they had been in touch with so many people outside of their family 'bubble'. As soon as this time was completed, Will returned to Leeds. The girls missed him. He had spent time with them thinking of fun things they could do while isolated at home.

'The Covid-19 virus will not go away any time soon,' he explained. 'Things may not seem too bad in this part of the country, but it is thought that Britain could get a second spike, especially in the Midlands and the North, where people are living at close quarters in larger towns and cities. I need to be back to help.'

'I'm starting back at work, too,' Dr Lacey explained to Song-Wei, 'but I'll be coming home to sleep from now on and I can take you to your appointments to have the plaster changed.'

It was hard for Song-Wei to sleep. She found the plaster heavy and needed help with so many personal things. But more than that, her mind kept going over the horrible experience.

'I hate those boys,' she said to herself. 'Why did it have to happen to me?'

The days in quarantine felt dark and bleak to her. All the good things of her time at Barrow House seemed to fade away and her mind just dwelt on the bad things, such as not being able to see her parents and grandparents. She thought about her guardian who had died from Covid-19, and that she had lost her connection with China. She worried because she would miss half of next term at school and might fall behind in her studies and lose her bursary. She was scared she might be a burden to Annelise's parents, and they would get tired of her being in their home because she was so miserable. Even when she tried to read her Bible and talk to God, He seemed so far away. Annelise was sweet and kept trying to cheer her up, but it did not work.

When it was her turn to make supper and talk about China, she felt so homesick that she left the table without finishing her meal, went upstairs and cried.

Mrs Lacey was quiet for a moment, thinking how best to try and help Song-Wei.

'Would you mind helping Dad clear up the kitchen?' she asked Annelise. 'I'm going up to have a little chat to Song-Wei.'

Upstairs, she gently knocked at Song-Wei's bedroom door. 'May I come in?' she asked.

At first there was no response, but then she heard a shuffle and Song-Wei opened the door.

'Sweetheart,' Mrs Lacey said gently, 'can we have a little chat? I can see you are very unhappy, and I understand that. You have been through a horrible experience and are coping with a broken ankle as well. However, I am your foster mum now and I really would like to try and help. If you don't want to talk now, that's ok, but I want you to know that I am always here for you and we all love you very much.'

Song-Wei allowed Mrs Lacey to hug her, but that made even more tears come.

She tried to talk, and between her sobs, explained some of her worries and especially how she hated the boys who had tried to harm her, and how she felt even God had deserted her.

When she had quietened, Mrs Lacey sat for a while holding her hand.

'Song-Wei,' she said, 'you are the one who has brought the love of God into our lives. I had forgotten Him and not talked to Him for years. Now my life has changed for the better because you taught me to pray. Uncle James and I intend to return to church as soon as it is open again. It may seem as if God has forgotten you, but He hasn't because He promises never to leave us or forsake us. You taught us that Bible verse, remember?

'When those boys attacked you, He used Goldie to bring help before any terrible harm was done. I think what has happened is you have forgotten that Jesus asks us to do something which may even seem unfair to us—and that is to forgive those who hurt us. While you hold hate against them, they are still causing you harm, but if you chose to forgive them, they will have no more power to hurt you. Do you understand what I am saying?'

For a while Song-Wei was silent. She thought about what her aunt was saying and remembered her dad had always taught her to forgive those people in China who made life hard for Christians, because it was a command of Jesus who had said to His disciples, 'You are my friends if you do what I command' (John 15:14).

'Thank you, Aunt Julia,' Song-Wei eventually answered. 'You are right. I don't want hate in my heart. I am sorry that I left the dinner table, that was rude of me. Please may I stay here and talk to Jesus? I want to get things right inside of me. Thank you for being so kind to me.'

Mrs Lacey hugged Song-Wei again and left her alone as she had requested.

A much happier girl appeared at breakfast the next morning. She had asked Jesus to take away her hate and anger and help her to love even her enemies.

– CHAPTER TWENTY-SIX –

China

Grandma and Grandpa Lee had settled well into their new home. With the help of physiotherapists who visited often, Grandpa was beginning to strengthen his leg muscles and able to stand and walk a little.

'I am so grateful to be alive,' he said to his wife, who was in the kitchen cooking the family's favourite chicken dish. 'But I am worried about our granddaughter. Who will pay her school fees now that Wong-Jong is no longer there to deal with the financial side of things? What will happen in the school holidays? Where will she go? Who will take care of her? She is still so young and now in a foreign country, without money or a guardian.'

'I know, dear,' answered Grandma Lee, 'and even though my concerns have been that you recover, never a day has passed without thinking about Song-Wei. England seems so far away, and I fear she might be treated as a refugee or put into a home for orphans. I cannot speak English and we have no way of finding out. After we have eaten, we will sit and pray about all these things. Jesus is near her in England, just as He is with Lydia and John in the Congo and us here in China. One day I feel sure we will all be together again.'

After they had prayed together, they heard a knock at their door.

'Whoever can that be, so late in the day?' thought Grandma Lee, as she hurried to open the door. Outside stood her supervisor, with a smile on his face.

'Sorry to disturb you,' he apologized, 'but in the mail bag today was a letter addressed to you, redirected from your apartment. I thought I would deliver it on my way home, and I want to check that you both are doing well in your new home.'

'Come in,' invited Grandma Lee. 'Can I give you some food? There is some of your favourite chicken dish still hot in the kitchen.'

'How could I resist that?' he answered, entering the house, and greeting Grandpa Lee. 'I see you are nicely settled, and I hope you have all you need?'

'Yes, thank you,' the couple answered. 'You have been very kind to us, we are so grateful.'

While he ate his meal, Grandma Lee opened the letter. It was from England, and inside, written in Chinese script, was a long letter from Song-Wei.'

'I can hardly believe it!' she exclaimed. 'We were sitting here praying for our granddaughter at school in England when you knocked, and here is an answer already in my hands. Praise God, He hears our cries!'

Grandma Lee was not able to read very well, but their guest read the letter out loud to them both. They were filled with thankfulness when they heard about the family who had taken her in, treating her as a daughter, and were interested to hear about all her adventures with her schoolfriend. At the end of the letter, she told them that she was sure now that she wanted to be baptized and take a Christian name. She had spoken to the minister of the church, who said it could be arranged when the Covid-19 crisis was over.'

The supervisor was interested as he read the letter to them. He asked Grandpa Lee what baptism meant, and he was able to explain to this kind man what it meant to be a Christian.

'I thought it was following a set of rules and philosophy which came from a foreign country,' he said. 'I had no idea that it was about a relationship with the Creator of our universe. I find that interesting. Maybe I can stop by and talk again with you about the Christian faith?'

'Of course, we would be delighted,' Grandpa Lee answered. 'You are welcome anytime, and to eat with us. I know you appreciate my wife's good cooking!'

Congo

Far from both China and England, another letter was being delivered. The small plane had landed at the airstrip, which would serve the small hospital in the forest. It was the day for the boss to inspect the progress of the building. John had driven the truck out to meet him and   collect the food supplies which he and Lydia had ordered, plus the private mail bag from China with letters for all the workers.

Lydia was waiting at the hospital to greet the supervisor, who wanted to brief her about her role now that the facility was about to open. She opened the mail and sorted it for all the different people. To her delight, there was a letter from her parents, one from Song-Wei and another from England which looked rather official. She looked on the back of the envelope, but the name and address meant nothing to her, so she tucked all their letters in her bag and went around the building site delivering the others to the workers. It was always exciting when the plane came in with mail and no one minded when they downed tools to read their news from home. Lydia was glad because that day nobody was disappointed. Everyone received at least one letter plus their pay packet!

Uniforms had arrived for her to wear in the hospital and it made her feel professional again, with an important job to do. She was really looking forward to being able to work as a nurse once again.

The hospital only needed a few finishing touches and a delivery of equipment, which was scheduled to arrive the following week. Once it was installed, the Chinese workers would return home—all except John and Lydia and a single guy who had chosen to stay and work as an engineer to make sure the equipment worked well, and to train up some local guys to be a maintenance team. An opening day was chosen, when the local people would be invited to hear about the services the hospital could offer, and the boss would hand over the hospital to the local area official. Some Congolese staff had been recruited from other hospitals, but it would take a while for local staff to be trained to do all the jobs needed to keep even this small hospital running well.

Once the plane had taken off, John returned to pick up Lydia. When they were back in their little home, she had time to open the mail.

There was so much good news. Song-Wei had written every week and a packet of four letters had arrived in a large envelope, sent first to Oicha hospital, then directed to them. They laughed and cried together as they read her daily journal but were so happy to know about the family with whom she was living through the lockdown. It was obvious that the Covid-19 pandemic was raging in parts of England and they were thankful she was in a safe place.

Then there was all the good news about Lydia's parents and the new home in which they seemed happy and settled. Lydia and John talked for a long time about the family and almost forgot there was still another letter to open.

– CHAPTER TWENTY-SEVEN –

Congo

The final letter from England came as a total surprise. It was from Wong-Jong's solicitor concerning her apartment in London, her personal belongings, and finances. Wong-Jong had left a will, stating that all she owned in this world was bequeathed to Song-Wei's family—to her and her parents, but to be administered by her father. The solicitor wished to be contacted as soon as possible, so that he could complete his work.

'I can't believe it!' said John feeling shaky from shock. 'This means we have a family home in London, and a lot of money in an English bank. I think we ought to make a journey to Uganda to get visas for a visit to England and from Uganda we can email this solicitor. I will talk to the boss on the radio tomorrow and see if we can take some leave.'

'I wonder if my parents would ever feel they could leave China and travel to Britain to see Song-Wei?' Lydia asked. 'If only they could speak a little English! I must write to them and pass the news on.'

'We have many things to sort out, but for now, let's just thank God for this gift. He must have given it to us for a purpose, so we need wisdom to know just what to do.'

The very next day John began to explore with his boss about a trip to Kampala, Uganda, followed by a holiday in England as soon as it could all be arranged. They would hope to return for the official opening of the hospital.

England

Song-Wei was longing to see her parents again. From the time Mrs Lacey had enabled her to join in the online services from the London Chinese church, she had been in contact with the Pastor, who gave his email address at the end of each service for people who needed help.

She emailed him about her family and asked the church to pray for them, and for herself following the death of her guardian. She also told him how the services had helped her and her wish to be baptized.

The Pastor and his wife then kept in touch with regular emails, encouraging Song-Wei.

Many of the members of the church had friends and family all over China, and the Pastor hoped that someone in the church might be able to make contact with Song-Wei's grandparents and let them know that the Chinese Church in London would pray for them all, including Lydia and John for their work in the Congo. From time to time the Pastor's wife phoned Song-Wei, and she loved having a chat in her native tongue—somehow it made her feel nearer to her parents and grandparents.

Miss Boston also received a phone call from Wong-Jong's solicitor, explaining the situation as regards the will left by her guardian. He had now heard from Song-Wei's father, that they had been able to arrange a short visit to London to finalize their affairs. As her parents were living in such an inaccessible place, Miss Boston asked if she could share this news with Song-Wei herself, so telephoned Barrow House to pass it on.

'May I speak to Song-Wei?' Miss Boston asked in an excited voice. 'I have good news for her.'

Mrs Lacey passed the phone to Song-Wei, who struggled to take in what she was hearing.

'They are coming to England?' she shouted in amazement. 'When? When will they arrive?'

'They are due to arrive at Heathrow Airport on the morning of 8 September,' Miss Boston told her. 'I have no more details, except that they will go to the apartment of your guardian and have to be in quarantine. Please pass me back to Mrs Lacey and I'll give her the contact phone number of the solicitor.

'I'm so delighted for you my dear. I hope your ankle soon heals and we look forward to you returning to school.'

'Wow! That's so cool!' said Annelise when she heard the news. 'I wonder how long they will be here? I hope they have time to come and stay with us.'

'That is amazing news,' said Mrs Lacey when she put the phone down. 'I can get the exact details from the solicitor. Once we know, we'll be able to make plans. I'll phone at once.'

'Aunt Julia,' asked Song-Wei, 'will I be able to go to the airport and meet them?'

'I'm not sure, Mrs Lacey answered. 'If you are, then you will have to self-isolate with them for two weeks. Let me find out more.'

Nothing much was done that day. The two girls were so excited, and Song-Wei was laughing, crying and dancing around as best she could with one leg in plaster!

It appeared that the solicitor was making all the arrangements needed for Lydia and John to be met and taken to the apartment, where they would stay until the quarantine period was over. He had bought a phone for them and gave the number to Mrs Lacey so that Song-Wei could phone and talk to them. He was a bit concerned as they only spoke limited English and there were so many rules to keep during the pandemic.

'I know what I can do,' Song-Wei said with a huge smile. 'I'll email the Pastor of the Chinese church and tell him where they will be and give him the phone number. Maybe someone can shop for them or bring them meals while they are self- isolating.'

'Fantastic. That is a brilliant idea!' Annelise said. 'Everything will work out well.'

- CHAPTER TWENTY-EIGHT -

Somerset

One evening in early September, Will organised a video phone call with the girls and his mother.

'Good news, he told them. 'I have traced a relative of Lucy Holm. She lives in Manitou. The records officer in Manitou found her and confirmed she is Susan Paulson's daughter, Lucy's granddaughter. Her name is Jayne Saunders, and she is a widow, 64 years old. She has twin brothers, Derek and David, who are 62 years old and still work the family farm on the prairie. Jayne is the oldest living relative and the person we should contact.

I was given an email address, so wrote and told her we have found some old letters dating back to 1730s, belonging to the half-sister of one of her ancestors. I have not mentioned the jewellery at this point. I think we need that to be verified and have a solicitor tell us if they would be the legal inheritors, since it came through Elspeth's half-brother. I'll let you know when I have a reply.'

'That's cool,' answered Annelise. 'We need to get the jewellery valued first. How are you doing up in Leeds?'

'I'm ok, thanks. I still get tired quickly, but glad to be back at work. We have a second wave of the virus up here and the hospital is gearing up to receive more very sick patients.

'How is your ankle, Song-Wei?'

'I'm doing well, thanks,' she answered, 'and I have good news of my family.'

She told Will the latest news and he was delighted for her.

'I can't believe that I will soon be able to talk to them and see them again!' she told him.

With home schooling restarting and hospital visits to check on her ankle, the time passed quickly and soon the day arrived when she received her first phone call from her parents. Song-Wei was so choked with emotion that it was hard to talk clearly but she was incredibly happy. There was so much to talk about, as she had not been in close contact for many months, and they chatted until their phones were running out of battery power. After that call, they were able to schedule a call every day.

'We are having our papers processed as soon as our time of isolation has finished,' her father told her. 'The Pastor of the Chinese church has been so kind, we have food delivered daily, and he has promised to organise the interpreters and legal advice we need. We are enjoying living in Wong-Jong's apartment, and so thankful to have a home of our own. I have been told that owning a home here should help our application to eventually become citizens.'

'You are going to stay here?' asked Song-Wei, in excitement.

'We hope this can be our base,' her father told her. 'The Pastor thinks I may be able to work with him after our contract in the Congo finishes, but that is a couple of years away as things stand at present.'

Mrs Lacey arranged to take a day off from her work and she travelled to London to see her friend who worked at the Victoria & Albert museum. They were able to meet in a park and sit at opposite ends of a bench, so that the friend could look at the treasure which the girls had found.

'I can't give you a definite figure as to the value, but it could certainly be worth several thousand pounds,' she told Mrs Lacey, who gasped out loud.

'As much as that?' she questioned. 'Without doubt, and having the letters and story will be a great advantage. My suggestion is that you put it in a safety deposit box until the Covid-19 crisis is over and, then bring it to the museum to be properly evaluated. It is a rare and beautiful set of antique jewellery.'

After they had chatted a while about the whole story and caught up on each other's lives, Mrs Lacey caught the train back to Bath. She followed her friend's advice and placed the jewels, along with the letters, in a safety deposit box at the bank as soon as she was able to do so. Once the pandemic was over, she and her husband planned to take the girls on a visit to Canada, but for the moment, that was a secret.

Once her plaster cast had been removed, and her parents' quarantine period had finished, Song-Wei was able to go to London and meet them. There was a 'rule of six' set by the government, which meant that Dr and Mrs Lacey and Annelise were able to go with her to London. They also had to meet outside, making it difficult for Song-Wei to contain all the emotions she was feeling—in Chinese culture it was not thought good to display emotions in public, but it was so very wonderful to be together again.

'We cannot say how we feel about your great kindness to our daughter,' Lydia told the Lacey family. 'We have prayed so much for her safety.'

'Your daughter has also taught us how to pray and we have been praying for you, learning of some of the difficulties you have faced as a Christian family in China. It has been a humbling lesson for us. We now pray for Christians in your homeland, especially those who have been detained by the authorities, and for people like Grandma and Grandpa Lee, who in their old age have risked their lives by helping in the hospitals.

Song-Wei translated this for her family, and her father smiled and replied,

'I once heard a wise man say that he had read in a poem, "Stone walls do not a prison make, nor iron bars a cage." We have learnt while in China that the pandemic has imprisoned people in differing ways and that, in the Congo, poverty and ignorance can be a prison, too.'

'Aunt Julia told me the words of that poem, too, and I have found that out, Papa,' Song-Wei said, looking at her parents with a huge smile on her face. 'And now you are here for my baptism. I want to be called Mary. Please come to visit us at Barrow House.'

'Yes, please can you come as soon as possible? How about this weekend? We fear that another spike of the Covid-19 is here and very soon and we may all be in another severe lockdown,' Dr

Lacey said. 'We know you need to return to the Congo, but we will be honoured to have you as our guests at Barrow House any time you wish to visit, so please come soon and spend as much time as you can with us.'

After discussions and a phone call to the Vicar at Summerfield, and to the Pastor of the Chinese Church—who agreed to drive her parents to Somerset—it was arranged that the following weekend Song-Wei would be baptized in the Barrow House swimming pool by her father and the Vicar. The Pastor of the Chinese church and his wife were also able to stay for the weekend and witness Song-Wei's declaration of faith and baptism.

As she came out of the water, Song-Wei was buried and Mary was filled with joy and so thankful to Jesus for all His love, and the love of her family and friends.

- APPENDIX ONE -

A nnelise's Potato Flour cake: very yummy and suitable for people who are gluten-intolerant, too.

Ingredients:

- $\frac{1}{2}$ cup of potato flour; 1/3 + $\frac{1}{4}$ cup of castor sugar; the juice and zest of a lemon or an orange; 3 eggs whites and yolks separated; small pot of double cream; 2 tablespoons of lemon curd

Method:

1. Whisk together the castor sugar, lemon/ orange juice and zest, and the egg yolks until the mixture trails a little on the beaters for a few seconds.
2. Whisk the egg whites in a separate bowl until stiff and fluffy.
3. Sieve the potato flour and fold in gently to the egg yolk mixture; then fold in the egg whites.
4. Turn into a greased and lined 7-8" baking tin and bake for 30-40 mins at 170 0C—160oC fan.
5. Allow the cake to cool and settle in the tin—do not panic if it seems to sink!
6. When cold: Take out of the tin and slice in two. Sandwich together with the cream, whisked until stiff, and mixed with the lemon curd.
7. Try not to eat it all in one sitting! Enjoy my favourite cake!!

Grandma Lee's easy-peasy Chinese chicken: This can be used to roast a whole chicken, or poured over thighs, drumsticks or chicken wings.

1. Mix together:

   ½ cup of dark soy sauce; 1 full tablespoon of runny honey; 1 full teaspoon of Chinese 5 spice; 1 full teaspoon of crushed or puree garlic; 1 full teaspoon of finely grated or crushed ginger; 1 full tablespoon of vegetable oil (I like sesame best, but any good oil will do).

2. Put the chicken into a dish and pour the marinade over it at least 2 hours before cooking, turning the pieces over from time to time.

3. Cook smaller pieces in hot oven, 200 oC or 180 oC fan, for 20-30mins; a whole chicken, cook as long as it takes to roast and for the juices to run clear.

4. Serve with rice or noodles and stir fry vegetables.

Everyone loves Grandma Lee's recipe!

– APPENDIX TWO –

We hope you liked this story—maybe it has made you think?

Here are some think boxes you could discuss with your friends:

1. Do you remember lockdown 2020? How did it affect you, and how did you feel?

2. What things did you enjoy about being locked down at home?

3. What things were hard for you to cope with?

4. Did you know that in some countries it is very difficult, and sometimes dangerous, to be a Christian? How can we help those people?

5. Annelise felt she was not clever or good at anything—Song-Wei felt she was born the 'wrong sex'. How do you feel about yourself? Do you believe that everyone is special and has some special talent? How can you find out what your talent might be?

6. Song-Wei had the courage to pray with her friends when they were in trouble. Do you believe that God hears our prayers and helps us when we ask?

7. After the attack, Song-Wei became depressed and angry, full of hate towards the boys who hurt her. Were her feelings putting her into a sort of prison?

8. Why is it important to face up to and to share our problems, fears, and negative feelings?

9. Song-Wei helped the Lacey family to find Jesus for themselves. Do you know Jesus as a friend who will never leave you on your own?

10. Song-Wei's father and Mrs Lacey both talk about the same poem. Do you think it is true that we can be imprisoned in other ways than being shut up in a building with iron bars? What might be stopping you from being free inside as well as outside?